Time On Fire

Jennifer Cole

Published by Trellis Publishing, 2021.

TIME ON FIRE

First edition. July 9, 2021.

Copyright © 2021 Jennifer Cole.

ISBN: 979-8224350407

Written by Jennifer Cole.

TIME ON FIRE

JENNIFER COLE

It was cold on the day of the funeral. Guests arrived covered in snow and ice. Laura stood at the front of the funeral parlor all day thanking people for coming to pay their condolences to her late husband, Tom. It was a closed casket. His death was far too gruesome for Laura to allow people to see. He was around fire almost every day, and it wasn't surprising that he burned to death after getting caught at the scene of a fire. He was always too brave for his own good. It's what made him a great firefighter, but it didn't always make him the best husband.

In fact, Laura and Tom were having problems before he died. He was not great at opening up, and it made communication a huge issue in their relationship. It was the main problem in their short four-year marriage. Laura just wanted to know what he was thinking and how he was feeling, but she felt so shut out. She told him over and over again that she needed to hear him say how he felt about her and their life together, but he just couldn't seem to express himself. Just hours before she learned of the horrible accident, Laura was on the phone with a divorce lawyer discussing the process.

Everyone held Laura and gave her sad looks. She felt guilty, and she felt like she didn't deserve the sympathy. If only these people knew what was really going on! If only they had seen him that one night they might look sympathetic for another reason.

Laura and Tom grew up together. They went to the same middle school and the same high school. They were in different circles in school, though. Tom was a part of the cool group. He dates gorgeous girls, and he was in three different sports throughout the year. Laura, on the other hand, was a bit more reserved. She was going through an awkward phase that never seemed to hit Tom. She had zits, and she thought that she was fat. She always had a crush on Tom, but she never had the courage to dare talk to him. They would smile politely at each other in the hall since they had known each other for so long, but that was it. Laura got much more confident after college. She lost weight, she felt accomplished, and she didn't have those darn pimples anymore. When she came home and saw Tom in his firefighter uniform, she wasn't afraid to go say hi. Two weeks later they were an official couple and about two years after that, they were married.

Looking back, Laura honestly couldn't remember why they got along so well. The physical attraction was definitely there, but she couldn't think of anything else.

"I'm so terribly sorry for your loss," a voice said.

"Huh? Oh, yeah. It's been quite a couple of days," Laura responded automatically.

"He was just so young."

"He was a very brave man. Thank you for coming."

"Well, honey, you know he's up there waiting for you."

"I like to think so. Yes."

The one thing that they don't tell you when you lose a family member is how darn repetitive it is. Laura couldn't actually say what she felt. She couldn't say that she was exhausted from making the arrangements, she couldn't say that she was bored of the funeral all ready, and she couldn't say that she was a tiny bit happy that it ended this way instead of divorce. She kept her grieving smile on, and she went through the proceedings like the mourning wife she was.

A young man who arrived by himself walked up to Laura and gave her a hug.

"It's such a travesty what happened," the man said. Laura was surprised by his affection. He seemed so touched by Tom's death. To be honest, it was the first time that Laura felt sad throughout the day. She wanted to hug him and comfort him.

"It was quite unexpected," Laura said.

"My name is Gary. I'd really like to get together sometime," the man said. "We both worked at the fire station. He was always the prankster, as you know. However, he had a big heart, too. I have a couple things that I"d like to share with you."

"That would be nice," Laura said. She never meant it.

When the day was finally over and she was able to go back home, the house felt different. It had a ghost in it. This used to be Laura and Tom's home. Laura and Tom's home didn't exist anymore, though, because Laura and Tom didn't exist. Their little suburban starter home was not filled with the hope and future plans that it once had. Laura tried to lay in the large king-sized bed, and she couldn't sleep. The next day, she put a For Sale sign in the front yard.

"And where are you planning to go?" Laura's mother asked when Laura told her the news.

"I don't know, ma. I'll go somewhere that I've never been. See things that I've never seen. Be someone that I am not."

"You can't run away from your problems, Laura."

"I'm not running away from my problems. I have nothing here for me. My job is a dead-end, and I don't have family or many friends. We moved here because this is the station that they assigned Tom. Now, I can go wherever I want. I have nothing holding me back."

"You make it sound like Tom was holding you back."

"You know that's not what I meant, ma."

"Well, you now you're always welcome back home if you need some time to figure things out. Your father is on the golf course almost every day, and I have my gardening. We won't be in your hair too much."

"I don't want to impose. Besides, I"ll be there in two weeks for Aunt Lilly's birthday."

"Well, take care of yourself, dear. I love you."

"I love you too, mom."

Laura sat down in her living room by herself with a glass of wine and a blanket over her. Her dog, Daisy, laid down at her feet sleeping. At least Daisy was there to help her feel less alone. It was a feeling that she was slowly getting used to. It was a feeling that was both terrifying and liberating at the same time. In a quick blur of just a couple of weeks, the house sold much more quickly than Laura anticipated, and the new family paid extra to move in as quickly as possible. Before she knew it, she had movers putting everything into storage temporarily, and she was off to who knows where.

*****

Laura sat in her car with Daisy in the passenger seat and a backseat full of suitcases. She tapped the steering wheel and looked around her with absolutely no idea of where to go. She was just blocks from her house, ready to leave her old life behind, but she didn't really plan for her new life that well. Eventually, Laura took a breath and started driving. She always liked Florida. She also liked Texas. There was Louisiana. Maybe she would go to Washington. Or Vermont. She liked skiing. Everything was so uncertain, but she just drove hoping to find an answer soon enough.

Laura drove for two days. She wasn't heading anywhere in particular, and she backtracked a bit. She spent nights in hotels and took breaks a couple of times a day to take long walks with Daisy.

Finally, she found a spot. She didn't even know what state she was in at first. She knew that she had been heading south for a very long time, and she was noticing the smell of barbecue and grass in the air. Everything was green, and there were more stars in the sky than she had ever seen. She was in a small town with a lot of small houses and shops. Everything looked old, and the roads were quiet. She drove around slowly looking for a motel or at least a diner. She could start looking for a house soon enough. Right now, she just wanted to get some sleep and some food and decide if this is where she wanted to build up a new life.

Laura found the Kentucky Suites on one of the main roads in town. It looked nice enough for her at the moment. She checked in. The room wasn't anything special, but it had a large, comfortable bed, a television, mini-fridge, ironing board, and it was clean. Plus, the facilities had laundry, an exercise room, a pool, and a hot tub. Laura decided that she was sick of driving aimlessly, and Laura paid for the room for a week in advance. She put away all of her clothes and sat in her room unsure of exactly what to do now. She knew that she should go explore the town and maybe start looking for a job, but she couldn't get herself to leave the hotel room. She ordered Chinese food and stayed inside thinking of Tom.

She hated Tom, but that didn't mean that he didn't consume her thoughts. Now that she was alone with her thoughts, all she thought about were the last days of her relationship with Tom. Laura found the text messages about a month before he died. Tom was sleeping and his phone continued to go off. Laura checked to see who it was before she woke Tom up. He was at the fire station for the last forty-eight hours, and she didn't want to disturb him. She decided that she had to wake him up when she saw who was calling him, though: his lover.

"Who the hell is Kathy?"

"Huh?" Tom asked groggily.

"Who the hell is Kathy?"

"She's a friend," Tom said. "I'm going back to sleep. I'm tired."

"Oh? She's a friend? Why is she calling you 'baby'?"

"What? I don't now, Laura. Jesus, will you let me sleep?"

"No. You better tell me what the hell is going on!"

"There's nothing going on, Laura. You're crazy!"

"Fine. I"ll just talk to her," Laura said. "I'll answer."

Tom jumped up from the bed and grabbed his phone from Laura's hand harshly.

"You will not touch my stuff without my permission!" Tom said. "There's no reason for this!"

"I'm not just going to let you cheat on me! I knew that we were having problems, but did it really have to come to this?" Laura asked.

"You're crazy!" Tom screamed.

Laura had never felt so horrible in her entire life. Was she not good enough for Tom? Did he not enjoy their sex together? Was the other girl prettier? Did he love the other girl? Was this the end of their family?

They spent the entire night arguing. Laura knew that he was cheating with the girl, but Tom refused to admit that he had done anything wrong. The fight went around in circles and circles. Laura started getting even more angry about Tom's refusal to talk. He tried to leave the room and the conversation every time that he got a chance. Laura would chase after him and try to get him to talk about the problem. He refused. The fight quickly turned into their repeated fight about his lack of communication. Tom left that night, and he stayed at a hotel. Soon, he came back, but they didn't talk. They lived with each other in silence. Tom would sleep in the spare room, and Laura would avoid him. The house became quiet. Dinners were quiet. They didn't bring anybody over.

Laura sat in her hotel room with take-out and tried everything she could to avoid the horrible thoughts filling her mind. She was still angry and still hurt. She hated Tom, but she missed him in the same way that she missed him before he died. Everything was so permanent now. She'd never be able to forgive him. She'd never be able to forgive herself.

*****

Laura woke up the next morning determined to move on. She was going to have to head out into town and start living her life again. She woke up, showered, got dressed, and she had some of the hotel's complimentary breakfast which consisted of orange juice, milk, coffee, muffins, and bagels. She went out into town to go explore, but she didn't really know where to go. She simply walked around to learn what was in town. There were a number of restaurants, stores, bars, and houses. It wasn't a big town, but it had a definite presence. The entire town was very country. It was new to Laura who had always lived in the suburbs. The air smelled cleaner, people smiled and waved, and people wore different clothes. They wore simple clothes, and children were playing outside instead of the kids in the suburbs who were on their computer or Xbox all day. Laura slightly cringed when she saw the firehouse in town.

Laura finally found a small diner in town and decided to get some coffee and read the help wanted ads in the paper.

"Hello!" a young woman smiled when Laura walked inside. "Will it just be you today?"

"Yes, ma'am," Laura said. "It's just me today." Laura was not used to going to a restaurant by herself. She usually had Tom with her, her mother, or one of her friends. She felt lonely.

"Well, come over here. Can I get you some coffee?" the young woman asked. She was a small girl who looked like she was barely out of high school. She wore jeans and a tee shirt with her apron.

"Yes. Please just a cup of coffee today, and I will take a local paper if you have it."

"Absolutely!" the young woman said. "Are you new in town? Or just visiting? I haven't seen you before."

"I'm new in town. Thinking of settling down here if I find the right gig," Laura said. "So here I am looking."

Laura sat down at the booth that the young woman had led her to and waited patiently for her coffee and paper. The diner was small, but it looked like a popular place for people in town to eat at on a Sunday morning. There were plenty of men and families scattered throughout the restaurant.

"Here you go," the young woman said. "Here's your coffee and your paper. My name is Jenny. I'll be back to refill your coffee in a little bit."

"Thanks, Jenny," Laura smiled. She opened the paper to the help wanted section, and she quickly realized that this was not the town for someone to get a new job. There were few opportunities, and Laura definitely wasn't qualified for most of them. She wasn't going to work in a warehouse or on a farm. She had a degree in English. That was when she saw the job opportunity for a high school teacher just one town over. Laura had gotten her teaching certificate because she figured it would be a good backup plan in case she didn't use her history degree for anything else. Laura ripped out the ad from the paper, and she finished her coffee picturing her new life as a teacher in a rural town in Kentucky. The more she looked around, the more she was liking the idea. She decided that she would spend the day sprucing up her resume, enjoy the hot tub and the pool, and turn in the resume tomorrow.

When she pulled up back into the hotel parking lot, she saw a familiar face by the entrance. She barely recognized him at first. It was the man who hugged her at the funeral. What would he be doing here? He seemed to recognize her, too. As soon as he saw her, he ran to her.

"You are not an easy woman to track down!" the man said.

Laura didn't know how to react. Why would he want to track her down so badly?

"Hi," Laura said. She was almost afraid. "I'm surprised to see you again."

"You know, you are beautiful. More beautiful than Tom ever described."

"That doesn't surprise me," Laura retorted. "He didn't really have a lot of appreciation for me when he was alive."

"I know that he did, though."

"Well, that's interesting because I never heard him tell me," Laura said.

The two were still outside of the hotel. Laura didn't appreciate where the conversation was going.

"Look, this is getting a bit heated. Let's go somewhere to talk," Gary said.

"And what do we have to talk about?" Laura asked.

"I was there the night that Tom died. I know that he'd like me to talk to you. That's why I was so determined to find you."

"Fine. There's a lake that I noticed down the road. We can go and talk there."

The lake was quiet. There was a gentle sound of water, and you could hear a cricket chirping every now and then. Laura and Gary sat down on the grass and both looked out at the lake.

"We were headed for divorce," Laura said.

"He mentioned that things weren't going that great," Gary smiled.

"Did he tell you the reason that we were going to get a divorce?" Laura asked.

"He mentioned that there was something going on. That he was talking to another girl and you found out," Gary said.

"That's a nice way to say that he's a cheating jerk. I'm only sad that he died before I was able to kill him myself," Laura snarled.

"I understand why you're angry, but it's over now. I also know he loved you."

"How could you possibly know that? Cheating on me wasn't a way to show me love. Refusing to talk to me wasn't how to show me love."

"I was with him that night."

"What night?" Laura asked.

"The night of the fire. It was one of the most horrible moments of my life. He was blockaded in the room. It only happened because the fire burned down a part of the ceiling and trapped him in the room. There was too much fire in between us. I wanted to help him, but he insisted that I had to get out before we both died. It was one of the hardest decisions of my life."

"I'm sorry that you had to go through that. You don't understand, though. Just because he was a firefighter who died in an accident, it doesn't take away from the pain from him cheating," Laura said. "It was horrible. I will never trust another person again."

"He wasn't cheating on you," Gary said. "He was talking to a friend about your problems. He couldn't open up to you. He was intimidated by you. He thought that you were brilliant, funny, and attractive. He was worried t hat if he talked to you that you would realize that he was beneath you."

"I don't believe you. If that was the case, he would have just shown me what he and Kathy were talking about," said Laura.

"He was a quiet guy. He wasn't really one to open up. You know that. Kathy is another firefighter, Laura. She's a lesbian. It was one of the only people that he could buddy up with and talk to."

"Imagine how it feels to know that your own husband can't open up to you," Laura said.

"He told me to apologize to you. He told me that he loved you. When he was stuck in the room, he told me to tell you that he loved you more than anything in this entire world. He apologized for not opening up to you. He said that he would be waiting for you," Gary said. Laura didn't say anything. "I know it was important to him for you to hear this, so I had to find you,"

Laura continued to stare out at the lake in silence. She didn't know how to respond. She thought that he was cheating this entire time. She started to feel an intense amount of guilt. Instead of enjoying their last month together, they barely spoke. Laura realized then that her last words to him were "those are mine" referring to the bottles of water in the fridge. Tears fell down her face.

*****

"Are you OK?" Gary asked, handing Laura a tissue.

"No," Laura said. "I'm not OK. I think that it was easier for me to handle his death thinking that he was a cheater. It's harder knowing that I lost a faithful and loving man."

"I know that you loved him too," Gary smiled. "He always talked about the little things you did for him. And the big ones."

"I wish that he would've expressed how much he loved me when he was alive."

"So what are you doing out here? I didn't take you for a country girl," Gary said.

"I never was a country girl. I'm really liking it out here, though. The air smells cleaner. The people are nicer. In the suburbs, the neighbors wave but talk behind your back. Here people are actually nice."

"This lake is quite pretty," Gary said. "They definitely don't have places like this in the suburbs."

"I know. Tell me about it."

"Why don't you let me hang out for a couple of days? I can help you get situated, and this way you will have someone to explore the town with," Gary said.

Laura couldn't deny that it was a tempting offer. She was lonely, and Gary could be a welcome distraction. She didn't know him, but there was something in his eyes and his face that made Laura trust him.

"Don't you need to work? They already lost one fireman," Laura asked.

"We have plenty of men on the force back home. I was thinking of helping out here for awhile. I can't imagine the fire station is too busy, but I thought I'd check and see if they need help."

"You would do that for me? I guess I could use the company."

"I'm doing it for Tom. The fact that you're beautiful and nice to talk to is only a bonus," Gary smiled. "Now, let's get out of here. I will check into the same hotel."

"I am thinking about going to apply at the high school in the next town tomorrow," Laura told him.

"Good. I"ll talk to the boys at the fire station when you do that."

Laura felt at peace for the first time in a long time. The town was so cozy, and she could live a comfortable and happy life here. It gave her a sense of relief to know that she could feel free to grieve since her husband wasn't a cheater. She lost her husband, but she didn't need to lose her happiness, too.

"This might work out well," Laura smiled. It was the first time that she realized exactly how cute Gary was. He had shaggy light brown hair and green eyes. He had large arms, and they were tattooed. He was a strong man, and Laura pictured him at the fire station lifting weights in his spare time.

Gary put his arm around Laura, and they looked out at the lake together in silence for awhile. The sound of the water made Laura relax, and she felt extremely safe in Gary's strong arms. Maybe this change of scenery was exactly what she needed. She didn't have the pitiful looks from everyone, and she wasn't constantly reminded of her old life. This place was full of new and exciting opportunities. Gary being there made it even better. He was respectful and warm. He was also the only person since Tom's death to make her feel better.

*****

When they were done talking at the lake, Laura and Gary went to the hotel to get Gary his own room. Laura was unsure of why Gary would be so generous to her, but she didn't care. She was just happy to have the help. She didn't want to admit that she was lonely and lost, but she was. Gary was also turning into quite a compatible friend. They enjoyed talking to each other, and she always respected firemen. She also thought that he could be quite funny at times.

They spent the rest of the night together. They found an Italian restaurant, and they worked out at the hotel afterward. They parted ways to their separate rooms afterward, and Laura almost invited him back into her room with her just for the company.

The next day, Laura went to the high school while Gary went to the fire station. The school was extremely receptive to Laura's resume. She had a good degree and plenty of experience. The principal said that she had not gotten anyone else nearly as qualified. The job was pretty much offered to her right there pending no problems with her references and criminal background. She walked out of the school realizing that she was starting a brand new life.

"Where are you?" Laura's mom asked.

"A small town in Kentucky. I'll send you pictures. It's absolutely beautiful."

"Well, I'm glad you went on vacation to clear your head. You have to get back into the swing of things now."

"Actually, mom. I'm thinking about staying here. I just talked to the principal of a local high school. I think I"m going to do that."

"Are you sure you want to stay in Kentucky for the rest of your life? You know there aren't any museums or theater there. I'm sure there are no nice restaurants. And you know how horrible teachers are treated, right?"

"Mom, like it here."

"But you're all alone."

"Actually, one of Gary's friends is here with me."

"Why would he come all the way out there?"

"He was here to make sure that I was OK after what happened."

"Well, that's nice." Laura could tell that her mother thought the situation was as odd as it was.

"Talk to you soon, mom. I gotta go."

Laura got back to the hotel and went immediately to Gary's room. He opened the door with a bottle of champagne in his hand.

"I don't know about you, but I will be starting at the fire station in two days!" he screamed.

"I start at the high school in a week!"

They embraced. Gary even picked Laura up a little bit. He opened the bottle of champagne, and they both jumped and cheered at the sounds of the cork popping.

"We have to celebrate. To a new life for you. To me honoring my commitments to my friend."

"Cheers!" Laura said, clinking glasses with Gary.

"Let's go out to the hot tub. It looks like fun," he said.

"Absolutely. I will go get my bathing suit on."

They were the only ones in the hot tub. It was still light out, and they stepped into the hot tub with the champagne.

"You know I'm really happy that you decided to come out. I was getting lonely," Laura told Gary.

"Fantastic. I'm glad that I'm making this easier for you. I can't imagine how it must feel to lose a spouse."

"It was one of the worst things that has ever happened to me. As angry as I was at him, he was the love of my life. It's hard to imagine that someone could be so kind and supportive. He always wanted me to be happy in whatever I did, and he was a great provider."

"I know he was a great guy. That's why I was so insistent on coming out here to see you. It's hard to lose a brother. It's even worse to practically watch it happen."

"Let's talk about anything else," Laura said after a moment of silence.

"How about us?"

"Us?"

"Yes. Us," Gary prodded.

"I don't know what you're talking about," Laura said nervously.

"I know that you feel it too," Gary said. "We have a natural attraction to each other."

Laura couldn't deny it. Gary was attractive and kind. She was starting to feel attracted to him. She started feeling it when they were sitting by the lake. He was so understanding, and she could actually talk to him. It was hard for her to admit her real feelings. However, Laura wanted to make sure that she wasn't just attracted to Gary because she was lonely and vulnerable after the death.

"I think that we should take it slowly," Laura said quietly. "I'm so far away from home. I also think that I'm going to stay here and take the job as a teacher."

"I will stay here too."

"Don't you have any reasons to stay back home? Family? Friends?"

"I have a bigger reason to stay here," Gary looked at Laura longingly. "You're so strong, and you're so beautiful. I want to be here for you. Who else would you have?"

"I appreciate your kindness, but I can do this on my own," Laura said. "I lost a husband, but I'm still relatively young. I also knew that this was part of the deal by marrying a fireman."

"That doesn't mean that you have to do it alone," Gary said.

"And what if you get hurt in a fire too? I don't think that I can go through that again."

"Look, it was my fault for bringing it up. I came here to tell you how much Tom loved you, and I've done that. Here, I'm starting to look like a prune. Let's get out of here."

"Yeah. I can actually stand to relax for the rest of the night. It was nice to have someone to celebrate with, though," Laura told Gary.

"We have plenty to celebrate. I'll still be here for a couple of weeks. I want to make sure that you adjust OK. You know what room I'm in."

With that, Laura got out of the hot tub and went to relax in her hotel room for the rest of the night.

*****

Laura and Gary stopped talking as much. They would get coffee in the hotel lounge in the morning and talk casually. They would also take Daisy out for walks together sometimes. Gary started at the fire station, and he loved it. The men were easy to get along with, and the fire station really needed him. His days were filled with rogue cigarettes igniting curtains. Laura was happy that Gary was able to help at the fire station while he was here. It was also nice to have a friend. The only other friend Laura had was Jenny at the diner.

The diner was one of the places that Laura started to feel comfortable in town. She walked in and Jenny immediately smiled and brought her a cup of coffee. Laura always went there when Gary was at the fire station in the morning. One particular morning Laura walked into the diner. Jenny was there as always.

"Hi!" Jenny waved. "I"ll go ahead and get you your coffee."

"Thank you!" Laura said cheerily, making her way to a small booth she liked to sit at.

"Are you gonna have breakfast this morning?" Jenny asked, putting down the coffee.

"Sure. I'm going to have a 2x2x2. Scrambled eggs and sausage," Laura said.

"Getting sick of the muffins and bagels at the hotel?" Jenny asked.

"Yes! It's fine, but eating here is so much better," Laura told her.

Suddenly, one of the guests at the diner got up in a hurry and ran to Jenny.

"I gotta go," he said. "There's a huge fire down the road, and they need all the help they can get. I need you to give me my tab now."

"Just go," Jenny said. "I will take care of this one for you."

"Thank you," the man said, and he ran out the diner and into his truck.

"My friend is at the fire station right now. I hope the fire isn't too bad," Laura said worriedly.

"Let me put on the news," Jenny said.

Laura followed Jenny to be as close to the television as possible and saw the huge fire on the news. A small house was completely engulfed in flames. The fire was the top story on every local news channel. Laura sat in fear watching the scene. Her mind filled with memories of Tom's death. She was filled with fear for Gary. She silently prayed for his safety and continued to watch for any new news.

The news went on to say that there was still one person left in the house. It made Laura sick, and she didn't want to watch anymore, but she had to make sure that Gary was alright. The story went on to say that there was still a person that they were trying to remove from the burning building. The following update advised the watchers that the person stuck in the building was a fireman.

Laura ran out of the diner without saying anything, and she drove to the site of the fire. She ran from the car, but she had to wait behind the caution tape and watch the action from a safe distance. She tried not to cry while looking for Gary. She didn't see him.

Finally, she saw Gary walking from the now smokey building with a small dog in his hands. He stayed in the building to bring the puppy to safety. Seeing him emerge from the building was the happiest that Laura had ever been. It was like she was watching Tom come back to life.

Laura ran past the caution tape despite the consequences and hugged Gary. He was in his fire suit, and he smelled like intense smoke. She didn't care what he smelled like. She was just happy that he was alive. She took off his helmet and kissed him. Happy tears fell down her cheek, and she hugged him again.

"I thought that I was going to lose you, too," Laura said into his large chest.

"I wasn't going to let that happen," Gary said. "I promised Tom that I was going to take care of you."

"You don't have to do that," Laura said.

"I know. I want to."

"What are you saying?"

"I'm saying that I have already told the fire station that I am planning on taking a permanent position. We can start a life out here together."

"Isn't it a bit too soon?"

"We'll go slow if you want. We can get separate places at first," Gary said. "Whatever you think is the best. I'm willing to go at your pace."

"Let's go. We can spend the rest of the day talking about our future together," Laura said.

"I can't," Gary laughed. "I have to complete the rest of my shift. I'll come see you as soon as I'm done with work. Now go on before you get us both in trouble. You're not supposed to cross the tape."

Laura kissed him one more time and went back to the diner.

"Where did you go?" Jenny asked.

"I had to go to the fire and make sure my friend Gary was OK."

"I knew that you were too invested in the fire," Jenny said. "I was going to find you at the hotel to give you your bill."

"I wasn't going to do that to you, Jenny. And you better get used to me. I think I'm going to be here for a long time."

Laura was one of the most popular teachers in the entire high school, and Gary became a quick captain at the fire house. The wedding was around the same time at a beautiful farm in the area.They moved into into a small three bedroom house and their first son was born about a year later.

ELAINE

Barbara Weisz

The train screeched to a halt and Elaine Sheldon had to brace herself for the onslaught of people trying to squeeze past out. Holding tightly around the handrail, she winced when a rushing man bumped his laptop bag against her hips, and she took a few steps back with the impact.

The man did not stop to apologize and Elaine only heaved a sigh and fixed her stance as the train resumed moving.

It was supposed to be a five-minute walk from the station to her apartment, but tonight, it did not feel like it. Her steps were slow and her shoulders were drooped. The streetlights refused to turn on properly and it flickered repeatedly as she passed by. Elaine sighed at the dreary atmosphere.

Just a week ago, these walks home passed by with a spring in her step, looking forward to the person who was waiting for her to be back, the person she had been going home to for the past six months, the man who welcomed her with a warm hug and a big smile after a tiring day at work—until the other day.

Her eyes felt heavy and the long wait for the elevator was not helping with her mood. She watched as the red arrow went down as minutes passed by until it reached the ground floor. Her ride back up was spent alone. She smiled bitterly. The world must really hate her.

All doors were closed when she alighted at the twelfth floor except for one. For a second, she almost panicked thinking that the opened door was hers, only to realize that it was the empty unit beside hers. Boxes are stacked in front of the door and the sound of a man's groans can be heard as she came closer.

She battled with herself if she should help or not. As the next-door neighbor, she knew she should, as a sign of welcome for the new occupant, but she also knew that the feeling in her chest is heavier than those boxes. She scoffed at her dramatics but looked down at herself. Her arms were already crying in protest with her handbag and laptop bag and those boxes looked nowhere near light so she forgot being thoughtful for once and unlocked her door. She was about to go inside when a man's voice startled her.

"Hi. Do you live next door?" The man beamed at her but the smile didn't reach his eyes.

Elaine smiled back, a closed-lip one. "And you must be my new neighbor," she offered her hand which the man accepted. "Elaine."

"Ivan. It's nice to meet you," he let go of her hand and gestured at the boxes. "I'll be done in a minute. You don't have to worry about the noises." He smiled again but Elaine can only see a grimace.

"Don't worry, take your time. I would have helped you but—"

Ivan waved his hand no. "No need. You must be tired from work," he observed, noticing the formal attire and the laptop bag hanging on her shoulders. "Go on ahead. Have a good night."

"You too," she returned in a clip tone and sent a brief smile again before going inside. The bang of the door echoed throughout the dark empty unit, reminding Elaine that she had no company anymore, that she had to spend the night alone in her empty apartment.

A tear escaped down her cheeks, which ended with bouts of sobbing for the third consecutive night.

—-

There are things in life that once you get a taste of, you'd never want to let go. And for Elaine, that was her relationship with Christian.

They started dating a little over a year ago, when they met at a mutual friend's party, though neither are close enough to the celebrant and her friends so they ended up chatting the night away. A week later, they found themselves agreeing to date exclusively.

Elaine did not have high hopes with her relationship at the start. Christian seemed to be the happy-go-lucky type of guy who always acted on a whim instead of having plans. She wasn't in too deep yet, so she didn't mind it at all.

But as the months go by and their relationship turned for the better, people around them started to notice—that Christian is changing for the good and it was mainly because of his relationship with Elaine. It flattered the female, she won't deny it. Knowing that she may be one of the reasons why Christian was trying to find a stable job, having the courage to pursue his passion in photography, and planning for his future, made her pleased.

All along, Elaine was expecting that she was included in the plan. It only dawned on her that she was never part of the picture when one day, she got home, expecting the smell of pepperoni and cheese for their usual pizza night, only to find a large bag filled with all of Christian's things that had accumulated in her home. They never agreed to stay together officially but they might as well be for all the days and weekends the male had stayed with her.

At first, she thought he was going for a vacation. She could've accepted it, a six-month out of the country trips to take images of the wonders of nature. What she didn't understand was why he had to break up with her.

They could've made it worked, Elaine believed so. She trusted herself to stay faithful and she put the same amount of trust on Christian. It just so happened that her ex-boyfriend did not believe in long distance relationships. It even hurt more when he said that he's not even sure if he's even coming back. His career was just starting, he said. It could be his one in a lifetime opportunity, he said. All Elaine could do was cry and beg him to at least try, but he was already decided.

And that was it. The end of a year-long relationship in just a snap.

—

The pastor was going through the sermon part and Elaine pinched her forearm to stay focused. They had to work overtime last night and she barely had a wink of sleep before she raced to be on time to the church.

Attending the mass was a weekly thing for Elaine. Christian never accompanied her no matter how much she forced him to and now, she's secretly grateful because at the least, she has this one activity she was used to doing alone.

The pastor's voice resounded against the walls and she snapped back into attention. Someone, a man perhaps judging by the black slacks and the scent, sat beside her. She almost rolled her eyes for the man's tardiness but bit her lips when she realized that she was no better for drifting off instead of listening.

The pastor droned on and she could hear the sound of the piano and the jingle of the tambourine but it faded as her lids became heavier.

By the time she woke up, people were standing up and were walking towards the exit. Elaine jolted in her seat, lifting her head from a sturdy shoulder she was leaning on, cheeks crimsoning due to the embarrassment.

She looked to her right and her eyes widened while the color of her cheeks got redder. "Ivan," she muttered. Of all people to fall asleep on while a mass was ongoing, it had to be her new next-door neighbor.

Ivan chuckled and raised his hand to his lip, which confused Elaine. When it dawned on her, she turned around and wiped the bit of drool that escaped her lips.

Clearing her throat and checking discreetly if there was still drool left, she turned back again to an amused Ivan. At least now, the smile reached his eyes unlike the first time she saw him.

"I'm sorry for falling asleep on you," she pursed her lips. An old lady passing by gave her a stink eye and she refused to shrink on her seat in shame.

Her neighbor saw the gesture and he chuckled. "It's okay. You went home late didn't you?"

"How did you know?" Her eyebrows furrow.

Ivan looked more amused now. "I heard your door. It wasn't exactly hard to when it's the dead hour of the morning," he explained.

Elaine nodded, laughing at herself for thinking of anomalous things such as Ivan being a stalker or a creep. It crossed her mind that it was still strange for him to be awake at such an hour but then that would mean it was also strange for her to have just come home so she didn't bring it up.

"Oh!" She unconsciously glanced over his shoulder and found a tiny, wet mark. Scrambling for tissues, she pulled a handful and wiped at his clothes furiously. "I am so sorry," she apologized repeatedly until Ivan had to hold her hand to stop her.

"It's spit. No big deal. No one's gonna die," he smiled once again. Elaine thought he should smile more often. It brightens up his face. Meanwhile, her face was on fire.

"Can I treat you for coffee then? As sorry and welcome?"

"I'd love to but I have somewhere to be. Maybe next time," he said noncommittally.

"Next time then." She apologized again before racing back home. A loud 'I'm home' is on the tip of her tongue but she stopped herself just in time.

Elaine dragged her feet to the sofa and flopped down unceremoniously with her legs hanging on an arm. Tears cascaded down her temples, which progressed into sobs. Her chest felt tight and her breath was constricted.

Earlier, she prayed to God to give her Christian back. She wished that Christian would change his mind and call her, or at least send her a message, saying sorry and that he wants her back.

She was praying but the pain hurt like hell. She asked God why did this have to happen to her, why she had to feel such pain, why she had to feel hopeful for her future for once, only for it to crumble right in front of her.

It was so unfair. She gave it her all but all she got was nothing.

—-

It had been a month since the breakup and Elaine was faring better. She haven't cried herself to sleep for two weeks now and she even had the energy to go out for a walk. It wasn't much but it was a start. She still thought of her ex-boyfriend from time to time, which was inevitable considering every corner of her apartment reminded her of him, but the pangs were getting less painful. In a way she didn't know how, she was getting by.

It was a Sunday and she was on her way to the church. A friend, Leslie, welcomed her with a hug.

"You're looking great, dear." The shorter female brushed her cheek against Elaine's and Elaine had to chuckle at her affections.

"Hi, how have you been? I haven't seen you here lately?"

Leslie beamed at her in delight. "I went on a vacation with Luis to France. Oh, we have to get some coffee later. I have lots of stories to tell you," she narrated giddily, the smile never wavering off her face.

"How's Christian? Still sleeping I bet?" Leslie chuckled and Elaine's eyes twitched. She swallowed a lump in her throat and an awkward silence passed before her friend realized that something was wrong.

"Hey, what's wrong?"

Elaine cleared her throat and forced a smile. "W-we broke up," she cursed at herself for stuttering. It felt more real every time she had to say it outloud and it doubled the sharp pain that coursed through her.

Leslie looked shocked beyond belief at the news and scrambled to wrap her arms around Elaine again. "I'm so sorry!"

Elaine, who had to fight the tears that were threatening to come out, hugged her back, glad to have someone to comfort her even if it was a month late. "It's okay. It's been a month."

She pulled back and wiped the tears that escaped despite her resistance. "I'm all right," she forced out a smile. Her friend looked at her worriedly but let it go for now. "All right, let's have lunch together okay?" Leslie asked, to which Elaine said yes. It had been a while since she had a meal with another person aside from her co-workers and she welcomed the thought now more than ever.

The mass lasted for a little over an hour and Leslie pulled her to a nearby Italian cafe that served great pasta and gelato. Elaine was grateful for the distraction but she could not help but glance at a table for two at a corner. She mentally sighed and erased the memories in her head.

—-

Elaine was working on a report when a call came. Not expecting anybody, she looked at her phone quizzically, which registered Leslie's name. Leslie rarely contacted her through the phone.

Surprised, she accepted the call and had to brace herself for a joyful Leslie who almost screeched a 'hello.'

"Hey, what's up?" Elaine reclined back on her seat and shut her eyes. She could hear her stomach grumbling only to remember that she didn't eat anything for lunch.

"I know this might be too soon, but it's been two months and it's not too soon right?" She said rapidly and Elaine had to sit up straight again and focus on her words to keep up.

"What exactly might be too soon?"

Leslie paused dramatically. Elaine could almost hear her excitement through the receiver.

"Dating."

"Dating?" Elaine repeated dumbly.

"Yeah, dating. I figure it's about time you meet new people. What do you think?" Elaine processed everything before saying an alarmed 'what' as a reaction.

She sighed before continuing. "Leslie, I know you have the best intentions in mind. But if you still didn't know, I barely have time to meet new people."

"But you have the time," Leslie insisted. "Every Sundays. Don't you always save your Sundays?"

"I do. But that's for church and some me time. I don't feel like going to a party or anything after a mass."

"Exactly. For church. And forget the me time, you have more than enough of that," Leslie paused and apologized for the insensitive remark, which Elaine only waved away. Leslie was just telling the truth.

"What I actually wanted to say is that I know this guy, from the church we go to, who you might be interested to meet," Leslie drawled on. It took a minute before it registered what she was suggesting.

"Are you setting me up on a blind date?" She asked incredulously.

"Uh, yes," her friend admitted sheepishly.

Elaine rubbed a thumb on a temple. "Do I have a say on this?"

"Not really. I already set up the time and date."

"Leslie—!"

"I had to! I know you're gonna say no!"

"Whatever. Just text me the details. I have work to do," Elaine grumbled. She heard a faint 'I love you' before she hung up the phone and she felt a little bad for not saying it back to her dear friend.

—-

That night, Elaine turned and tossed on her bed. She couldn't stop thinking about the blind date and she had bombarded herself with too much questions that only left her more confused and doubtful.

Is it too soon? What if Christian knows about it? What if the guy isn't what she's expecting him to be? But then, what exactly are her expectations?

The fact that he goes to her church is a good point, but the thought that she saw it as a good point gnaws at her guilt. It might be ridiculous but she felt guilty for indirectly saying yes to the blind date. It had been two months but thinking of a possibility of a relationship with anyone other than Christian brought a bad taste to her mouth.

—-

Elaine pushed the glass door open before a waitress assisted her to her seat. A man was already seated at the table, but she could not see his face yet.

A gasp escaped her lips when the waitress stopped and gestured at their table, making the man look up.

"Elaine?" Ivan said, sounding shell-shocked himself.

"You're Leslie's friend?" Elaine asked for good measure. She had not seen her neighbor for weeks now. The last time, they only exchanged brief hellos when they happened to meet while taking out trash.

Ivan stood up and helped her pull her seat back, before returning to his own side.

"And you are Leslie's friend," Ivan jokingly deadpanned. Elaine took her seat and began to chuckle. Ivan, amused by the situation, also began to laugh.

"I guess we'll be having a date today?" He asked with a smile on his face. Elaine hummed in affirmation while smiling from ear to ear.

"How did you meet Leslie?" Elaine asked once their food was served.

"I actually knew Luis first. He was an old friend and he was the one who suggested this place for me to move to," Ivan explained before taking a bite of the grilled chicken.

Elaine took a sip of water before responding. "Why did you move? Was it for your job?"

The question froze Ivan for a second before he relaxed. Elaine bit her tongue for the question which obviously hit a nerve.

"You don't have to answer it if you don't want to," She said softly.

"Sorry," he offered a timid smile.

"It's okay," she smiled before diverting the conversation to a different topic.

It turned out that they have a lot of similar interests than they could have expected. They have the same fascination with the Harry Potter series, the same geeky side when it came to Star Wars, and the same passion when it came to football—though Elaine loved Man U with a passion while Ivan preferred Chelsea.

Hours later, they found themselves laughing comfortably around each other while they walk together home. They stopped when they reached Elaine's door and Ivan kept a good distance, to which Elaine was grateful for.

"I really had a lot of fun," Ivan smiled.

"Me too. I think it's been ages since I've laughed that much," Elaine gushed.

He put his hands in his pant's back pockets and Elaine mentally chuckled.

"We should do this again some other time?" It was more of a question rather than a statement.

Elaine let out a deep breath she didn't know she had been holding and nodded. "Sure."

—-

She threw the frame inside the black plastic bag and flinched at the sound of breaking glass. Next were the t-shirts and boxers that were definitely not hers, followed by other toilet utilities that were never meant for a woman.

It was a day after her blind date and last night, she had the urge to throw away everything that reminded her of Christian. It had been months but she still kept some of his belongings that he left there, silently holding on to the hope that he would come back.

This move did not mean anything but a sign of her trying to move on. She had been meaning to do it for weeks but the date with Ivan was the last push she needed to start working on it. She sniffed and sobbed for the first few minutes but it got better as the plastic bag got fuller.

It was filled with pictures, letters, dried flowers, candy and chocolate wrappers, and almost every single thing that Christian gave her during their relationship, including the bracelet that he gifted to her last Christmas. It took a lot of emotional effort but afterwards, she felt lighter, as if an invisible baggage was thrown away.

The door next to her opened just as she was pulling the plastic bag outside to throw it in the bin. Ivan looked as surprised as she was. He was sporting a shirt paired with loose shorts and running shoes.

"Going for a run at night?" She asked, eyeing his outfit.

Ivan shrugged. "The park's good enough for some laps."

Elaine stopped for a second to think before taking a leap of faith. "Mind if I join you?"

—

The night was a bit chilly but fortunately, there was minimal wind.

Elaine had been living in that neighborhood for years but it was the first time that she jogged at the park. She always thought it was full of rowdy teenagers getting drunk or creeps who had nothing better to do with their lives. Ivan laughed at her when she voiced it out.

"This place's actually good," He panted, arms swinging as they jogged around the vicinity. "You should just avoid Friday nights because it can be too crowded."

She looked at him curiously. "How long have you been going here?" She asked, breaths coming short. Ivan slowed his pace a bit.

"Since the first week I moved," he answers. "It was a bit lonely staying indoors."

Elaine stopped in her tracks, causing Ivan to stop too.

"I am so sorry for being a very unwelcoming neighbor. I should have made you something and came over to check on you."

Ivan rested a hand on her head and ruffled her hair. Elaine felt like pulling away but didn't, surprised at how large his hand felt. "No need to feel sorry. I know it wasn't your best day then," he continued jogging and she followed automatically.

She gulped as she remembered that day. It was definitely one of her most miserable days. "Yeah. My boyfriend just broke up with me a few days before that," she chuckled dryly. This time, it was Ivan who stopped first.

"I am so sorry to hear that."

She pursed her lips in thought. "It's okay. I've been doing great. It wasn't an excuse to not welcome you," she patted his shoulder, signaling him to continue moving.

It was silent for a few minutes before Ivan spoke up again.

"I just got divorced a few months ago."

Elaine screeched to a halt. "What?" Her eyes widen at her rude reaction. "I mean, when?"

"A few weeks before I moved," Ivan looked down. "My ex-wife and I just got divorced and I realized I can't stay at our home for long so I sold it, and moved here," he gestured at his surroundings with feigned enthusiasm. "And I think I made a great decision."

Elaine took a step closer before wrapping her arms around him. "I am sorry to hear that."

She could feel him shaking his head as he hugged her back. "I guess we're both sorry to hear about each other's heartbreaks?" he joked to lighten the mood. She pushed him back and hit him lightly on the chest before laughing.

They both broke into fits of laughter, earning the questioning looks of the passers-by.

—

They continued to contact each other throughout the week. They may be neighbors but Elaine frequently opted to work until late night so they can't really meet much. Leslie called once to check on how the date went and squealed when Elaine responded with a simple 'Thank you' and shouted 'I knew it, I knew it' repeatedly until it burned Elaine's ears.

The following Sunday, Elaine and Ivan agreed to go to the church together, causing Leslie to get excited upon seeing them.

She looked at them knowingly and winked at Elaine, who blushed at her friend's action. Ivan chuckled at the sight but pretended that he did not see it. All of them, including Luis, Leslie's boyfriend, sat side-by-side inside the church.

During the mass, Elaine prayed and asked for guidance, if what she was doing was right or if it was too soon to consider liking a different man. When she opened her eyes and looked at Ivan's direction, she found him to be staring back at her.

She glanced away and fought down the blush that crept on her cheeks.

—

It was a Wednesday night and usually, Elaine would still be at work, doing things that were not really urgent.

When she got home, it was way too early for bedtime and she found herself thinking of the man living in the unit beside hers. Curiously, she laid an ear flat on the surface of the wall to check for any noises. She didn't know why but she wanted to check if Ivan was home.

She could hear a faint sound of music and she thought about it once, twice, and multiple times before deciding to send him a message.

A few minutes later, there were knocks on her door. Elaine, already clad in more comfortable clothes, welcomed the sight of Ivan carrying chips and soda.

"Did you bring any DVDs?" She helped him bring the things to her living room and settled them on the coffee table. Ivan reached for his back and pulled out some cases and handed them to her.

She raised her eyebrows at the choices. "So you're basically suggesting we watch the whole series of Harry Potter?" She looked at him pointedly.

Ivan shrugged before making himself comfortable on the couch. "Pretty much," he grinned.

In the middle of the movie, they found themselves sitting close to each other, shoulders almost bumping. Elaine looked at her side and it was only a few inches away from Ivan's. Unconsciously, she continued to stare until he looked back.

"Like what you see?" he grinned mischievously, earning a smack on his chest.

"Your scar," she started, pertaining to a small scar at the left corner of his lips.

"Ah, they're battle scars," he jested. Her forehead scrunched at the vague answer.

Ivan sighed before reclining fully. "I had a bit of a scuffle last year. I saw my then wife with another man and I confronted them right on the spot. And the rest is history," he smiled but the bitterness was pronounced.

Elaine copied his position and leaned her head on his shoulder. It was a bold move and she was holding her breath if the male would shrug her off. However, Ivan lifted his arm and rested it on her shoulder so she could scoop closer. Elaine let the tension seep out of her body.

"I only have one question," she said after a while.

"What is it?" He closed his eyes, hoping that he could answer it whatever the question was.

"He got it worse right? I mean, you managed to hit his face at least twice? With bruises?"

Ivan burst out laughing. "Yes, yes, I did. I kicked him in the stomach, too. It was pretty satisfying," he answered, still chuckling at the unexpected question.

"Good," She said before placing an arm over his stomach.

They watched the rest of the movies in the same position.

—-

Elaine was typing her report when her boss approached her.

"I read your latest report, about the success rate if the company decides to venture in e-commerce." She waited with bated breath. It was a report she had been working extra hard for.

"And I can say I'm impressed. I sent a copy to the higher-ups and we just have to wait for their comments," he patted her on the shoulder.

Elaine beamed and said thank you.

"You should continue doing what you've been doing recently," he commented, puzzling Elaine.

"I mean, you look happier. Whatever the reason is, continue doing it," he said before turning back to his office.

Elaine could only think of one big change in her life recently. Biting her lips to stop herself from grinning too widely, she smiled at the thought of a man.

—

She was preparing the TV and the player for their usual movie night when Ivan received a call. His expression dimmed and his jaw locked when he saw who was calling but still answered it, walking towards the kitchen for some privacy.

Elaine, though worried, stayed where she was and fiddled with her own phone. She tried to give Ivan the privacy he needed but was surprised when his voice got louder.

"I don't give a fuck about it. I'm deleting your number. Please don't call me anymore."

She could hear the sound of a phone hitting the floor and she scrambled off the sofa to check on him.

Ivan was staring at the broken device and his chest was heaving deeply. Slowly, she walked towards him and reached for his shoulders. He relaxed at the touch and rubbed a hand on his face.

"I'm sorry you have to hear that," he reached for her hand and pulled her closer to him before hugging her waist.

Elaine put her hand on his hair and carded her fingers through the black strands.

"It was my ex-wife," he explained, making Elaine halt her actions for a moment. She only resumed when Ivan nudged her hand with his head. "She was telling me about her wedding in two weeks, and that I'm invited." He laughed bitterly. "She cheated on me and she had the guts to invite me to her wedding."

Elaine, now shaken, fought the tears that are threatening to spill. She can feel the hurt from Ivan's voice and it was affecting her more than it should.

She remained silent, listening to Ivan's breath until he completely relaxed and his breaths evened out.

The silence was deafening until Elaine had the courage to break it. "Do you still love her?"

It was a yes-no question but Ivan didn't respond for the next two seconds, nor even for the next minutes.

Feeling defeated, Elaine pulled herself from his grasp, ignoring his pleas to make her stay. She collected her things from his living room before walking her way outside and into her own unit. Ivan knocked on her door for a few minutes until she said from the other side.

"Please. Stop it. I need some time alone."

The knocks stopped, and a few seconds later, another door was shut.

—-

Just months ago, it was Christian who was the cause of Elaine's sleepless nights. It was him who was the reason why she cried and continuously asked herself of what's wrong with her and why do people find it so hard to love her. It was him who was the reason why she didn't want to wake up to face another day and tempted her to just laze on her bed, feeling as if all the energy had been sucked out from her.

But now, just a few months later, Ivan had been occupying her mind much more than she expected he would.

He is a good man. He's nice, funny, responsible, smart, and even good-looking—a complete catch if she dared say. When she first saw him, all sweaty and panting from carrying heavy boxes, she just saw him as just another attractive man who happened to be her neighbor and nothing else. Admittedly, she even forgot about him until their embarrassing encounter at the church. That was how it was, but because of one date, it turned into something more.

Elaine found herself genuinely enjoying Ivan's company as they spent more time together. It started from scheduled dates and movie nights until they found themselves into a routine of being together every other day, whether it was to just talk, share about their day, or watch movies.

It was a routine that they easily adapted too—they never forced themselves into it nor did they set fixed days and to-do lists whenever they meet. Day by day, Elaine found herself thinking of her ex-boyfriend less, and whenever she did, it was to smile at the memories they shared and never to wallow in the sadness and the gaping hole he made when he left.

As Ivan made her feel light-hearted, carefree and secured, she found herself forgetting about the heartbreaking nights, about the times when she went back to an empty home, and about the thrown away pictures and gifts. With Ivan, she felt that she could try again, that she could, maybe, fall in love again.

But it seemed that Ivan thought otherwise. She could still see how hurt he was when he talked about his ex-wife inviting him to her wedding. She could remember how tightly clenched his fists were and how much he was trembling in anger. It was a sight she never expected to see from the usually composed man.

When she asked that question she wasn't hoping for an absolute no. They were married and she knew that he must have felt so strongly for her to ask for her hand. But at the least, she was expecting something along the lines of 'I'm doing fine' or 'I'm getting over it' and it would have sufficed, for her at least.

If anything, it made her realize how much she was wearing her heart on her sleeve yet again. She wasn't in love with him, not yet at least, but she knew she was on her way. All along, she thought he felt the same, that he was moving forward and trying to forget his past heartbreak, just like her. Elaine thought that a part of him had thought about her in a romantic way, that she might be someone who he can ideally like, but then again, those were just Elaine's assumptions.

The problem with her, as always, were her hopes and baseless assumptions. These always manage to fuck her emotionally—big time. She just never learned.

—

Ivan tried to contact her in the following days but she was resolved on avoiding him for a few days. She was aware that she was being immature but she deemed herself unprepared.

Every day, she recited every line she could say once they managed to talk. She imagined different scenarios and how she would react to them and what she should say. She admitted, most of her though-of situations were bad. She wasn't too hopeful that they would be returning back to the friendly yet flirty camaraderie they had formed.

Elaine was far from being level-headed. When it came to feelings, she was like an open book. She never tried to hide what she was feeling nor did she ever lie about it. So when one day, while standing on the train, hand clasped tightly on the handrail, and a man stood behind her and asked "Will you be my girlfriend?" she broke down in tears and attracted the attention of other commuters.

Among all the scenarios she imagined in her head, this wasn't how it was supposed to be. He wasn't supposed to show out of nowhere and tell her things she has been wishing to hear for weeks in the middle of a crowded train. She tried to stop her tears but the various emotions overwhelmed her.

Ivan had panicked, wiping away her tears furiously with his fingers and then the sleeves of his sweater. He was expecting her to shriek or push him away or to give him the finger, but this wasn't in his imagined reactions.

When the train stopped at the next station, he gently guided Elaine out and continued hushing her. Her cries were now reduced to sobs and Ivan cursed at himself for making her cry.

Once she was calm, she smacked him hardly on his chest, before saying a garbled "Yes."

For a while, Ivan was confused why she said that but broke into a large grin when he realized the implication.

Overjoyed, he grabbed her face with both hands and kissed her, right in the middle of the station, with some bystanders looking away from the scene. The kiss was chaste yet sweet. Their lips glided smoothly against each other and for a while, Ivan was tempted to press harder, which was futile when Elaine pushed him.

"But," Elaine sniffed and shushed him with a finger on his lips. "Explain."

"Could I take you home first? It's starting to get cold," he gestured at her working clothes—a thin blouse and a pencil skirt—and led them outside and hailed a cab.

There was a deafening silence throughout the ride home and their way up in the elevator, but Ivan never let go of her hand the whole time.

He led them to his unit instead of Elaine's and she was about to protest but he insisted.

He pushed her until she was seated on the sofa and he sat beside her as closely as possible. She squirmed in her seat and he gave her some space, rubbing his neck sheepishly.

He reached for her hand and turned his body towards her.

He started with a deep breath before launching to his long narrative. "That night, when you asked me if I still loved her, I was sure that my answer was no," He brought a hand up when he saw that she was about to interrupt him.

He continued once she silently agrees to keep on listening.

"But at the same time, I can't say it. It sounds more real once you say it out loud doesn't it? Am I making any sense?" He chuckled. Meanwhile, Elaine responded that yes, she understands because she felt the same thing with Christian.

"We were a couple since high school, and then through college. Most people called us the ideal couple and were just waiting for us to get married. It was as if there was no other way out of it but to build our own family. So I did ask for her hand in marriage and she said yes." Ivan heaved a deep breath, composing his next words in his mind.

"But as soon as we started living together, something felt...weird. A year later, I realized how used we are to being together. We were so used to seeing each other, to doing things together that it only seemed natural that we got married. I realized that maybe, we took marriage for granted, and it was a hurried decision merely out of obligation because of the people's expectations."

"We started to drift away from each other then. In the back of my mind, I knew she was thinking the same thing. When I saw her with another man, it hurt me—not because I still love her but because I was at least expecting that we wouldn't reach that point where we would hide secrets behind each other's backs—especially a lover at that."

"I saw red and then I found myself furious. I was angry at her but more at myself for letting us be trapped in that situation. When we decided on the divorce, it was heartbreaking but it felt like a burden

I never knew I had was lifted from me. It felt liberating." He paused, tightening his hold on Elaine's hand. Elaine returned the gesture, egging him to go on.

"I admit. It still hurts. But not because I still love her but more from the fact that I spent so many years thinking I was happy but realized that I wasn't. It was hard coming to terms with that: that I forced myself to think that everything was alright when it wasn't. And then suddenly, she told me the news that she's getting married and practically screaming at me that she's found her happiness. I'm happy for her. We've been together for so long that I can't even bear thinking of hating her. But then I thought of myself and my sorry state of a coward who can't even ask you to be mine and I was enraged because I felt that it was unfair. I thought that I deserve my own happiness too." His voice trembled then and he blinked repeatedly as his eyes began to get misty.

Elaine knelt beside him and pulled his head to her chest, rubbing his back consolingly at the confession.

"I'm sorry if I hurt you. Because all these just came crashing on me and I suddenly couldn't answer. I didn't know where to start. It felt too much." She felt a wetness on her arm and hugged him more tightly. If she could only take a part of the pain he was feeling, she would do it.

"I'm sorry for assuming the worst, and for not giving you a chance to explain." She muttered, kissing a spot in his head to reassure him that she was there, and she won't be leaving anytime soon.

Ivan retreated and pulled her into his lap, resting his forehead against hers. "I'm sorry for giving you the chance to assume the worst, then. If anything, I just really want to say how much I like you and how much you make me happy." He gave her a peck and kept his lips there, feeling the smile forming on his lips.

"I'm really glad I met you. I'd do anything I could so you could forget him completely."

Elaine shook her head no in protest. "No, Ivan. We will work together so we could heal completely. This is no you helping me, nor me helping you. This is us helping each other," she said, gazing into his eyes lovingly.

He smiled a smile that reached his eyes, the one that Elaine absolutely adored, before replying. "I love the sound of that."

SUNRISE, SUNSET

FELICE ROCKWELL

43

Iris Quinn's body lay nearly comatose on the cold, sterile bed at Boston General Hospital. She had skipped her insulin doses in recent days, and her diabetes was out of control. She believed that medication was too expensive and a waste of money on someone of her advanced age. She didn't see the point. Except for a couple of acquaintances and the caretaker who went to her home a few times a week, she had no one left in the world. She was lonely and ready to move on from her earthly existence.

"We're losing her," Dr. Patel shouted in an exasperated tone. "I'm not getting a heartbeat on the monitor. Get the paddles," he ordered.

Iris saw her lifeless body below her as her essence seemed to drift up from her form. She felt no distress as she watched the medical personnel fight to save her life. She was caught between two worlds. She was filled with a sense of peace. All at once, Iris found herself back in time as memories of times past filled her vision.

The year was 1947, a couple of years after the war had ended. Nineteen year old Iris stole away for a moment from her duties at her family's Italian restaurant to read a few stanzas from a book of poetry she had been immersed in.

Working in the restaurant wasn't her favorite thing to do, but she knew she fared better than so many who had to work in factories during that time. The restaurant named for her grandmother yielded her family a comfortable lifestyle. It was one of the more popular eateries in the small suburb of Boston.

Iris's grandmother, who was known by everyone as Nonna, started the restaurant when her daughter, Sophia, was a teenager. The three women were on their own as both Nonna and Sophia lost their husbands in each world war. Iris never really knew her father.

"Iris! Table eight has been waiting for you to take their order."

Sophia was loving, yet firm with Iris. She knew Iris often had her head in the clouds. The past few years were difficult, and Sophia understood Iris's desire to escape into her make believe world. However, Iris needed a dose of reality from time to time.

"Yes, Madre," Iris complied.

Iris lay her book down and went to greet her patrons.

"It took you long enough. We haven't got all night," said the female diner, unleashing her fangs on Iris.

"Uh, it's quite ok, Miss," interjected the male companion.

Iris was instantly attracted to the gentle Irish brogue of the man at the table. She couldn't help but notice he was handsome as well. He was a good ten years or more Iris's senior, but had a boyish charm about him. His dark brown hair was longer at the front and top; it was slicked to one side and held it in place with pomade. His light blue eyes seemed to smile along with his thin lips, which formed a slightly crooked grin.

"The special this evening is Veal Marsala," Iris informed them. "Of course, we have our regular menu items as well."

"I think the Veal Marsala sounds quite scrumptious," the Irishman told Iris as he nodded to his lady friend.

"Actually, I would prefer something more agreeable," the female companion replied testily. "I'd like something besides veal." She spoke in a vain and haughty manner, and seemed contrary to Iris. It was clear the woman would find fault with most anything.

"I'll have the Chicken Parmigiana," the lady said, almost barking her order to Iris.

Iris noticed throughout the evening that the gentleman seemed bored, and at times embarrassed by his female companion. She felt sorry for the Irish gent. She also felt relieved when they departed the restaurant so that she wouldn't have to put up with the woman any longer. She wouldn't have minded, though, listening to the male diner speak a little more. She fancied his accent. She imagined how wonderful it would sound to hear him recite some of the poetry in her book.

The next morning, Iris went out to the courtyard that was set to the side of the restaurant. They grew herbs in the courtyard for many of the dishes served in the restaurant. Flowers lined the paths as well and provided fresh blossoms for the tables of the restaurant. An old cast iron bench rested alongside the Marian statue that Nonna had brought with her from Italy. Iris took breaks as she cut herbs and flowers and laid the fresh bunches in the basket at her feet. The breaks afforded her opportunities to catch up on reading.

She opened her book of T.S. Elliot poems and continued to read where she had left off from the evening before, on Elliot's work, *The Wastelands*. She transcribed the German words from part one of the poem:

"Fresh the wind blows
Towards home
My Irish child
Where are you now?"

Her reading was interrupted by a familiar voice. The Irish gentleman from the evening before approached her from the street.

"Good day, Miss," he said to Iris as he tipped his hat. "I wanted to apologize for the rudeness of my companion last evening."

"Oh, really, it's quite ok. I'm sure your wife just had a bad day or something," Iris replied. She was surprised to see him again.

"Oh no, Miss. She wasn't my wife. My pal set us up for a date. I guess you can say it didn't go over very well."

Iris noticed it again. His slightly crooked smile was adorable and as charming as his accent.

"I'm Alister Quinn. I've just come from Ireland a few months ago. I'm the new editor at the Boston Herald, and I live in the flat just across the way there," he informed Iris as he pointed to the apartments not too far down the road.

"My mother and Nonna, my grandmother, own this restaurant. We live above it so I suppose we're neighbors," Iris said. "My name is Iris."

Alister noticed the book Iris was holding in her hands. "Perhaps you would like to accompany me to dinner near the harbor one day, and we can discuss his poetry," Alister said.

"I would like that very much," Iris agreed. She was intrigued that a man would consider her insight. "Sunday evening would be best," she suggested as the restaurant kept her busy most days.

It would become a ritual that the two of them would meet on Sunday evenings. They quickly became inseparable. They would steal moments during the week, usually with Alister sitting with her for a few minutes before work, on the garden bench. Their courtship lasted nine months. At last, Alister asked for her hand in marriage.

"*Mo Ghrá Eternal*?" It had become a term of endearment from Alister to Iris meaning *My Eternal Love*. They had just finished reading sonnets from Shakespeare. "Would you do me the honor of becoming Mrs. Alister Quinn?"

He had knelt down in front of the bench, and his fingers clutched a ring which had been his grandmother's. The ring was like none Iris had ever seen, fashioned in antique silver. Two hands held a heart with a crown on top, and there was an emerald stone inside the heart. *Mo Ghrá Eternal* was etched on the inside of the band.

Alister had already received a blessing from Iris's mother for Iris's hand in marriage. He was a proper gentleman and would have asked her father, had he still been alive.

"Yes," she shouted. She wanted nothing more at that moment. Iris couldn't be happier ...

"We have a heartbeat," Dr. Patel emphasized as he instructed the nurses to pause their efforts. Their mission was accomplished. Iris drew back from the brink of death.

She again found herself supine on the table at Boston General. Her body, her consciousness, whatever - she didn't know what had happened. She had relived one of the happiest moments of her life, but here she was, thrust back into the present.

She couldn't open her eyes, but she could hear everything around her. She was disappointed to have left her other state, whatever it was. She felt the weight of her body and the sorrows of her heart settle upon her once again. Unable to speak or move, she was not really troubled by it, and time passed without her notice.

****

With time, Iris came out of the diabetic-induced coma and was transferred out of ICU into a step-down room at the hospital. Dr. Patel had assessed her. He determined that the only lasting damage from her diabetic episode was to her eyes. Iris could no longer see very well. Everything was a blurry mess, and she couldn't focus on anything.

"Alright now, Mrs. Quinn. We have you all settled in your new room. My name is Nurse Douglass. If you need anything, here is the call button." She took Iris's hand and placed it over the device.

It was a scary and frustrating experience for Iris. Not only was she ill and alone, but having her vision so impaired just made matters worse. Now more conscious and aware, she felt her mood darken.

Iris guessed that Nurse Douglass was an African American woman, based on her warm voice tone and the texture of her skin when the nurse had grabbed her hand. During their initial, brief encounter, Nurse Douglass reminded Iris of her caretaker, Janice, whom Iris was quite fond of. Iris wondered if Janice or anyone had checked on her during her days in ICU?

"Code Blue to Room 214. Code Blue to Room 214." The loud call for help from the intercom jolted Iris, and she felt more frightened. She heard the frantic pacing of doctors and nurses rush past her door into a nearby room. She could see only shadows of the figures hurrying to answer the code.

The voices of the medical personnel faded into the background as Iris felt panicked.

"You'll get used to it after a while," a male voice promised.

Iris had not noticed anyone else in the room before.

I must be in a semi-private room, she thought to herself. She found it strange that they would place her in a room with a man rather than a woman. She noticed a shadow to her left which she suspected was a curtain used to provide more privacy.

The voice reminded her of her beloved, Alister. She detected a faint accent which sounded Irish, but the gentleman's voice was softer and older than Alister's.

"Are you well enough to read?" the gent inquired. "It could help take your mind off of things while you are here."

"I'm...I can't see very well anymore," Iris informed him. "I'm losing my vision." Iris's voice sounded weak and frail.

"I can read to you, if you'd like," the man offered. Iris nodded in appreciation.

The gentleman read from a book of poetry which included many of the famous poets of the nineteenth and early twentieth centuries. He read her some of Keats' work, as Alister had so many years ago.

"Bright star, would I were stedfast as thou art—
Not in lone splendour hung aloft the night
And watching, with eternal lids apart,
Like nature's patient, sleepless Eremite,
The moving waters at their priestlike task
Of pure ablution round earth's human shores,
Or gazing on the new soft-fallen mask
Of snow upon the mountains and the moors..."

Iris relaxed, the gentle readings calming her troubled spirit. The voice of the gentleman remained eerily familiar. Though she was entranced by the words he spoke, the medications took over her tired body, and she fell asleep as his voice faded into the night.

***

The next morning, Iris awoke to the sounds of the morning medical staff making their rounds. Nurse Douglass arrived into Iris's room to tend to her needs.

"How are we feeling this morning, Mrs. Quinn?"

Iris shrugged one shoulder and reluctantly nodded. She wasn't sure how to answer.

"Well, I suppose I've been better, dear," Iris responded.

Nurse Douglass checked Iris's blood sugar.

"Hmmm... Still elevated a bit," she said with disappointment. "We're going to have figure out what to do with you," the nurse said as she exited the room.

The day seemed so long to Iris. She wondered what would become of her life. How would she manage when she left the hospital? Would she even leave the hospital? There were so many questions and so few answers.

She tried to pray away her fears, but felt so weak and afraid. The gentleman in her room sensed her distress and offered to read to her again.

"Psalms always helped to calm my beloved wife's fears. Would it be okay if I read them to you?"

"Please." Iris was thankful to hear the elder man's voice again.

> *"Even when I walk*
> *through the darkest valley,*
> *I will not be afraid,*
> *for you are close beside me.*
> *Your rod and your staff*
> *protect and comfort me."*

The words comforted and soothed Iris's weary soul. She remembered how she and Alister read verses from Song of Solomon on their wedding day. She told the story of her love for Alister to the stranger on the other side of the curtain.

"We were married on St. Patty's Day. Alister and I had both been raised Catholic and attended the same cathedral down the road from us, but somehow had never seen each other until the day when he came to our restaurant. Perhaps it was because my Nonna always insisted we arrive a half hour early prior to each service. She ushered us to the very front pew as though the spot was reserved for us. She would say that to be at the very front was like being at the feet of God."

"I wore the same wedding dress that my Madre had worn to her wedding. Nonna styled my black hair and clipped a large hair comb to the front side of my head. The comb was very beautiful and very old. It had three large sapphire stones, and Nonna said it was a perfect match for my blue eyes. She said the two together looked like the waters of the deepest ocean."

"My Alister was dashing as ever. I couldn't take my eyes off of him as I walked down the aisle. I wish I could say that I remembered what he wore, but I just remember his tilted smile and his eyes. We did not glance away from each other. Our eyes were fixed in anticipation that I would soon be Mrs. Alister Quinn."

"We read verses from Song of Solomon in our vows to each other. It had become an almost nightly ritual that we would recite excerpts from the book, so it seemed only natural to include them in our promise to each other."

"My beloved has gone down to his garden,
To the beds of balsam,
To pasture his flock in the gardens
And gather lilies.
I am my beloved's and my beloved is mine,
He who pastures his flock among the lilies."

"The church spilled over with people. We were popular in our district of Boston. Everyone knew our restaurant and had dined there, so there were many guests there to wish me well. I always felt sad for my Alister because he had a few of his friends and mostly people from the newspaper, but he had no family to speak of there to bless him in his new life. He never really shared with me why. I suppose I should have asked. I always figured, perhaps, that it was too expensive for his family to come to America."

"Perhaps it was enough for him to be where he was with you and your family became his family?" The gentleman had interrupted Iris's narrative of her life with Alister.

"Maybe," Iris conceded. "I hope we helped to fulfill his life. I know he did mine."

The gentleman smiled and nodded at Iris, and though she could not see it, she sensed it.

Iris continued with her story of her new life with Alister.

"Madre and Nonna prepared all of the food for our reception. It seemed only fitting to receive the wedding guests at our family restaurant. We had plenty of room to accommodate everyone, and extra tables were set outside in the garden terrace. Oh, it was so lovely. The wedding was in late May and all of the spring flowers were bursting at the seams."

"Our reception was lively and entertaining. Alister had sung with a couple of other Irish lads in the pubs they ventured to before our courtship. He'd often serenade me with songs from his homeland."

"When I told him his eyes smiled at me just the same as his crooked grin, he introduced me to the song he would eventually sing at our wedding reception. It quickly became of favorite of mine and it was *our song*. He managed to work up the courage to sing it to me in front of all our guests, and as he did, he twirled me around the dance floor."

Iris began to faintly sing the chorus to the song she had heard Alister sing to her often. With her weakened voice, it was more of a whisper that filled her hospital room.

"When Irish eyes are smiling,
sure 'tis like a morn in spring.
In the lilt of Irish laughter,

you can hear the angels sing.
When Irish hearts are happy,
all the world seems bright and gay,
And when Irish eyes are smiling,
sure, they steal your heart aw..."

Iris's voice faded. She had used all of her strength during the emotional recounting of her life. She felt somewhat breathless and tired, and panted a little. Nurse Douglass walked into her room just in a time to catch a glimpse of Iris's struggle to take a deep breath.

"Mrs. Quinn! How long have you been this way?"

"Not very long dear. I think I just excited myself."

Nurse Douglass checked Iris's oxygen levels. Her frown deepened as she fit the oxygen mask over Iris's face.

"Try to take a few deep breaths."

The nurse felt Iris's wrist and took her pulse and blood pressure. She felt satisfied that Iris was stabilizing after a few minutes of oxygen.

"I'll be in to check on you more often this evening. In the meantime, remember the call button is there for a reason," she reminded Iris as she wrapped Iris's hand around the cylindrical apparatus.

The nurse gave Iris more of the medication that made her sleepy. She drifted off once again.

***

Iris grew more tired in the coming days. She wondered if the man who had kept her company all those days in the hospital was still with her in the room.

"Hello," Iris called out. "Are you still there?"

"I'm here," the elderly chap acknowledged. "I think they want you to remain calm, so I didn't want to disturb you."

"Rubbish," Iris said. "Maybe I'm too weak to talk much, but you can talk to me. I want to know more about you."

"I'm not sure where to start," the old guy told Iris.

"Why don't you start from the beginning?"

"Well, I was a wee boy in Dublin."

Iris knew it. His accent wasn't as robust as Alister's, but it resembled it still the same.

"I lived with my Nanna, who was my Mum's Mum. My Mum and Pops struggled to make ends meet while my Nanna watched over me. God rest her soul. She was a good part of my life when I was younger, she and my Mum. But Mum's life was hard."

"Pops worked hard, but we couldn't seem to get anywhere. He was upset all the time and drank a lot. The more he drank, the meaner he got."

Iris's new friend paused.

"I don't think I should be telling you this. I don't want to upset you."

"No, please. I want to hear about it," Iris said. "Go on."

"When my Pops wasn't drinking, he could be the kindest man. But when he was drunk, things could get out of hand. He'd hit my Mum, sometimes he'd hit me. My Mum or my Nanna often got between Pops and me to protect me."

"One night, he was smoking in the chair and fell asleep. The chair caught fire and burned the house down with it. My Mum and I made it out, but Nanna and Pops died in the fire. I had a small cloth sack with a couple of treasures in it that my Nanna had given me that I always wore around my neck. I always had that to remind me of her. Everything else was destroyed in the fire."

"We stayed with relatives until my Mum found a way for us to be on our own. It took a while, but she did. Mum always found a way. I never knew what she did then, but I have my suspicions now."

"It was pretty rough, growing up in Ireland. It was a beautiful place, but it was filled with so much turmoil. I was good in my studies and worked to better myself. I always said I would be a better man than my

Pops, and if I ever was blessed with children, I would never treat them in a bad way. And if I were ever fortunate enough to find the love of good woman, she would save me from the wretched life I came from."

"Somehow, I made it to America and was determined to start a new life. After school, I worked my way up at my job, and became successful. But I still had a hole in my heart. I wanted someone to love and to love me."

"One day, I found her. I found my angel, and we got married. And.."

Iris had fallen asleep again. They had her on stronger medications, and she didn't have the strength to fight their effects.

Nurse Douglass had come in to check on Iris regularly. She was growing fond of her. She noticed Iris had relaxed her grip on the call button and went to move her hand near it again. She noticed the beautiful Claddagh ring around Iris's finger.

"Something tells me that your life has a story, Mrs. Quinn," she whispered as she pulled the covers higher over Iris's tiny and shrunken body.

***

Despite their best efforts, the doctor still struggled to gain control of Iris's diabetes. One problem would be solved, but the medications often complicated another. It was an exhausting process for both the doctor and Iris.

A few days turned into weeks at the large hospital. Iris continued to sleep a lot. Each time she awakened, she wondered if her roommate was still there. And each time, he was.

"Last thing I remember was you telling me about your hardships in Ireland," Iris told her friend. "I know much of what I've told you of my life has seemed idyllic compared to yours. But I want you to know, you weren't alone in the tragedies of life. Alister and I experienced our heartbreaks as well."

She could see the shadow of the man move closer to her. She couldn't make out any distinguishing features. Her eyesight had grown worse in recent days, and she had very little vision left.

"Let's see. Where did I stop last time?" she asked.

"You had just gotten married," her friend reminded her.

"Oh yes," Iris acknowledged.

"Alister and I moved in a place just across the way from the restaurant, but I still helped my Madre and Nonna. That is until..."

"Until?" The man echoed after Iris paused.

"Until our son, Danny, was born." Iris had a strange look on her face. It was one of many emotions, as if she wasn't sure which she should feel.

"When Danny was born, our lives changed. I had not known how complete a child could make our lives. We had already felt complete when we found each other, Alister and I. But a child brought something to our hearts that we didn't know was possible. We loved someone much more than ourselves. At last, I understood my Madre and Nonna."

"Alister doted on our little Danny. Alister wanted to name him 'Danny' in honor of his grandmother. He said she'd sing the song, *Danny Boy*, when Alister was sad or afraid."

"Alister was a lot more hands-on than most fathers of his time. He'd steal away moments from work early in the afternoons to get home and spend more time with our little Danny. He'd read to him, fly paper planes he had made for him, and he'd tell him that one day, they would fly across the world together. He did all sorts of things. Of course, he sang to him too. I guess you know which song he sang," Iris said as she chuckled and felt alive for a moment.

"One day, our lives were turned upside down. America was in the midst of the polio epidemic, and despite our best efforts to keep him safe, our Danny got it."

"He was seven years old, and one day couldn't get out of bed. Alister had taken Danny to fly a kite just the day before. He was so excited when had come home from their day in the wide open field. I remember him running through the garden gate and yelling 'Madre, Madre! Papi and I flew the kite into the air. It went so high! Almost as high as the clouds. You should have seen it!'"

"I remembered thinking I would go with them next time. There would always be other times, so I'd thought. The next morning, our little Danny was paralyzed down one side."

Iris began to weep with what little strength she had. Her roommate made tiny whimpering sounds as well.

"Save your strength," he cautioned her, his voice breaking slightly. "I think we need to let this rest for now."

Iris had no choice. Remembering the devastating moment in her family's life had taken all of her strength.

Nurse Douglass came into her room and saw that Iris had been crying.

"Oh my word! What's got you all upset, dear lady?"

She dabbed Iris's cheeks with tissue and brushed her thinning gray hair back away from her worn and wrinkled face. The compassionate nurse put her hand on top of Iris's hand and told her "Iris. I have you on my heart each day when I come in here and each day when I leave. I don't know what God's plan for you is, but I know this."

Nurse Douglass put one hand under Iris's and clasped the top of her hand.

"He's got you in the palm of His hand. It will all be okay."

Iris once again was quick to fall asleep after getting her medication.

Nurse Douglass felt bad for her. During Iris's stay, she had only noticed one visitor and that was early in Iris's treatment. She was too sick then to notice or remember. Nurse Douglass was told it was Iris's caretaker, but the visitor had not returned.

How sad, Nurse Douglass thought, *that anyone should be that alone.*

***

During her next moments of lucidness, Iris continued to tell her story to the man she could sense was only a few feet from her.

"At first, the polio didn't affect Danny's breathing much. He had spent a good bit of time at the hospital learning how to walk again. He could walk some, but it was easier for him to just be in a wheelchair. So when he came home, he was more confined than he had been before polio took over his body."

"Alister had built ramps that helped Danny get around better. Otherwise, he tried to treat Danny much like he had before he was sick, although perhaps was a little more overprotective. Alister would carry Danny out to the field so that they could fly kites. During days when the winds were kinder, he'd hand Danny a reel and help him hold it in his hands as they flew the kite. I went with them on those days. I had learned every moment was precious, and nothing could be taken for granted."

"Winter had come, and the doctors somehow felt the cool air would help Danny feel stronger and aid in his recovery. So, they would have us sit him out in the cold air a few minutes on days that we were able."

"We were always cautioned that Danny had lungs that were weaker than they should be because of the polio and that a small cold could set him back and even force him to spend time on an iron lung to be able to breathe."

Iris took a deep breath, exhausted in her tale of her son's health crisis.

"Influenza was spreading through Boston as was a massive snow storm. Everything was shut down. It was hard to get from one place to another. The flu was hitting whole families at a time, and it made its arrival to our house. It knocked us all down, but no one was harder hit than our Danny. We wanted to get him to the hospital, but it proved to be nearly impossible. Transportation was down. Communication lines were down. And we barely had the strength to walk from one room to another. Still, Alister and I took shifts at Danny's side, while we waited for conditions to improve. We had planned to get Danny to the hospital as soon as we could."

Tears fell from Iris's small, bloodshot eyes. She thought she heard the sound of a whimper come from her friend. They had grown very close and seemed to feel each other's pain. There was an unspoken bond which developed between them. There was even a love they felt for each other as they spent many hours in the dark hospital room.

"I walked into Danny's room, and Alister was sobbing. He was cradling our Danny's lifeless body and rocking back and forth. He wept until he could no more and then just stopped rocking, almost as if he was frozen in time."

"I had nearly collapsed on the chair on the far side of the room, unbeknownst to Alister, who was deep in his grief. Somehow, I managed to get myself up. I walked over to the two people I loved most in the world and wrapped my arms around both. It was my time to sob as I lost control of my emotions. And as I did so, Alister started singing the song he had sung to our son from the day he was born:

'Oh, Danny boy, the pipes, the pipes are calling
From glen to glen and down the mountain side
The summer's gone and all the roses falling
It's you, it's you, must go and I must bide
But come ye back when summer's in the meadow
Or when the valley's hushed and white with snow
It's I'll be here in sunshine or in shadow
Oh, Danny boy, oh, Danny boy, I love you so
But when ye come and all the flowers are dying
If I am dead and dead I well may be
You'll come and find the place where I am lying
And kneel and say an 'Ave' there for me...'"

Iris's friend had joined her in recanting the song by now, both gently singing barely above a whisper.

"And I shall hear tho' soft you tread above me
And all my grave will warmer, sweeter be
For you will bend and tell me that you love me
And I shall sleep in peace until you come to me."

"We cradled our son amidst the deafening silence that followed. We couldn't seem to will our bodies to move for what seemed like hours. Eventually, we did. I couldn't tell you when or how long we lay there on the bed with our son."

Iris grew silent. Her companion was silent also. No more words were spoken that evening in the hospital room, until at last, Iris drifted off to sleep.

***

The doctors were running out of options for Iris. They couldn't seem to get her diabetes under control, and there were signs that she was losing kidney function and declining rapidly.

In spite of it all, Iris felt no worse than she had been feeling. She was anxious for the conversations she had with her friend. Somehow, she felt he knew her heart and was able to glimpse at her soul.

"Eventually, it was time to move on without our Danny," Iris continued the story.

"You couldn't tell me that at the time. The loss of our little Danny nearly ended me. I locked myself away in my room, and stared out of the window into the distance."

"Alister tried to reach me in all sorts of ways. He would read sonnets of our favorite poetry. He would sing hymns or read verses from the Bible, particularly Psalms or Song of Solomon as he had always done."

"It fed my soul and somewhere within the depths of my being, it made me feel alive. But I didn't have the strength to pull out of my grief just yet."

"Alister never gave up on me and eventually, I came around and started living life again. It was a life without Danny. One day I realized poor Alister had to live it too. I had been selfish in my grief and had shut him out. It was time to try and move on. Alister saved me from myself. He saved me from the depths of despair. I don't know if he ever knew it, but he did."

"I have a feeling you saved him as well," her faithful companion told her.

"I don't know," Iris questioned. "When I think about it, there was so much I didn't know about his life before me and I should have asked. I was an open book."

"Maybe his life started when he met you," the old man reasoned. "Perhaps that is so?"

No one had been so encouraging to Iris since her Alister. She found herself once again comparing the similarities between her new friend and the love of her life.

If only for a brief moment, she felt young again and wondered if it was too late for love once more. She quickly put the thought out of her head. She was nearing eighty, and she would never allow herself to love another besides her beloved, Alister. She had a number of chances after his death, but always remained faithful to their love.

"Mo Ghrá Eternal - M'aingeal.."

Iris couldn't have heard what she just thought she did. *Maybe I'm hallucinating*, she thought. It was the voice of her friend using the terms of endearment that Alister had spoken to her on an almost daily basis. *Mo ghra eternal, M'aingeal* which translated meant *My Eternal Love, My Angel*. No one had ever spoken those words to her except for Alister. Iris couldn't recall telling the gentleman in her room about that. She questioned herself over and over again. She was on a lot of medications. Maybe she didn't remember telling him? Still, it was a bit unsettling.

"Did you just say something," she asked him.

Nurse Douglass walked in as Iris was speaking.

"Who are you talking to dear?"

"I was just asking my friend over there a question," Iris responded, still feeling a bit shaken.

Nurse Douglass's eyes widened, and she looked perplexed.

"Hmmm... There is no one here my dear but you and I," Nurse Douglass told Iris.

Iris gasped. "No! It can't be true. Why are you saying that?"

"It's ok Mrs. Quinn. Just calm down. We'll..."

Nurse Douglass noticed Iris's body grow limp. She checked her breathing and heartbeat and both were absent from Iris's body. She hit a button and called the code.

"Code Blue, Room 210, Code Blue, Room 210!" shouted Nurse Douglass as she started CPR on Iris.

Iris discovered herself again looking at her body from above. This time, there was a light and on each side were two figures. She moved closer to the light. She recognized the figures. There to take her home were Alister and Danny. There were no words spoken, but a language between them that transcended beyond the human comprehension. Iris's spirit knew then that the stranger in her room was her Alister, comforting her and preparing to take her home.

THE END

ANNALIESE

Elizabeth Martone

Annaleise rolled over in her cotton sheets and stared out the window at the sun beaming through the ragged curtains of her bedroom. The light from the morning lit up the interior of her modest room. The cock crowed as she stirred and stepped from the comfort of the warm bed. As her delicate toes touched the floor she winced at the feel of the cool floorboards beneath her feet. She mentally prepared herself for another typical day in the remote Amish community where she was raised. She sat on the edge of her bed and began braiding her long, golden locks. Her hair had never been cut. Once finished she tied a tiny, white bow at the end. Standing up, her hair extended all the way down to her upper thighs.

From the homely bedside table, she grabbed her prayer cap, the white cap made of organza and stiff with starch that she must wear in public. She slipped it over her long, golden braid and stood, making her way over to the wardrobe, barefoot. The floorboards creaked beneath her slender frame. The house in which she lived was in need of much repair, but it was home.

Her dress was bound by the Amish community to which she belonged. She pulled out the calf-length, gray dress, and her white apron to accompany it. She looked the outfit up and down, sighing at the restrictions she had to abide by. Just a little color or a little lace would make it so much more tolerable, but alas it was forbidden.

She slipped the dress over her head, atop the white, cotton undergarments she wore beneath. Her slender arms penetrated the long sleeves at the ends and her delicate fingers stretched out toward the floor. Her blue eyes reflected in the full-length mirror that stood opposite. They ran over her entire frame, assessing the modesty of her attire. Her smooth legs peeked out the bottom of the gown. Her hands just protruded from the sleeves. How she longed for something different. To have somewhat more choice when it came to the little things. But living here her options were overly restricted. With a sigh, she turned away from her dull reflection.

Her stomach growled lightly, alerting her that breakfast time was upon her. Before leaving, she quickly raced to the window and opened it wide, allowing the cool morning air to hit her face. It almost stung as the contrasting wind nipped at her warm skin. She turned on her heels and made her way to the exit of her humble sanctuary, ready to start the day ahead.

Before opening the door she took a deep breath, hearing the faint clip-clop of hooves outside. She felt a tear well up in the corner of her eye, but she willed it to stop. No matter how much she tried, Annaleise was overwhelmed with pain with any reminder of her parent's accident. No day since their passing had her parent's death become any easier for Annaleise. Each day she was reminded of the terrible accident they had undertaken. As soon as she set eyes on the cart outside, laying rusted and disheveled. Unused for a year. A constant visual scar, sitting in their front yard. Although she knew that her brother, Jacob, shared her pain she would not dare discuss with him.

He had been walking down the street when it occurred. On his way back from the cornfields down the road from their home. Their mother and father waved as they passed, smiling at him. The next thing Jacob knew, he was watching their cart overturn as the horses bucked and bolted, leaving the two bodies trapped beneath the wreckage. Around him, people screamed at the sight, but all he could do was rush over to find his parents laying lifeless in the middle of the dirt road.

Annaleise was distraught. She cried for weeks. She took to her room and moped. No one could comfort her. Since then the community had done their best to assist the two orphaned children. They stayed in the family home, but here they could barely make ends meet. Her job as a milkmaid at the dairy farm and his as an apprentice blacksmith left them living pay day to pay day. They relied on handouts from neighbors and friends to feed themselves. Still, Annaleise and Jacob vowed to take care of themselves, and that was just what they did. Regardless of if it was against the rules.

One evening, months after the accident, Jacob had an idea. He weighed it up in his mind over and over. He had promised Annaleise the day of their parents passing that he would always take care of her. That was just what he intended to do. But not if it meant risking her safety or standing within the community. Finally, he decided that there was no other option for them. The need for financial stability was too great.

"Come out with me tonight," he had asked, his voice trembling with what she felt to be nerves, excitement or worry, she could not distinguish.

"To where?" she had asked, but he would not answer. Annaleise was wary at first of her brother's sudden plan. Still, she trusted him and so she followed, through the woods and to the city on the other side.

"Where are we going, Jacob?" she asked on their journey. He turned and held out his hand, signaling her to stop in her tracks. He opened the knapsack he had been holding tightly to his chest since they had left the community. Inside was a range of colorful clothing, the likes of which Annaleise had never seen.

"I am taking you to the city," he explained, pulling out a pale pink fitted dress and white heels for his sister. She stared in awe at the strange fabric garments handed to her.

"You need to wear these, otherwise they will know we are not from there," he explained. Entering a modern city in their modest attire would surely give them away as patrons of the well-known Amish district just miles away. Jacob had experienced this prejudice first hand after all.

"I will stand over there. Let me know when you have changed. You can put your clothes in this bag," he gestured to the bag from which he had pulled the new outfit. Then he turned and walked out of sight, giving his sister the privacy to change.

She untied her apron and dropped her dress to the forest floor. She folded them and placed them in the knapsack Jacob had provided. She shivered in the cold night air. Picking up the new dress she pulled it gingerly over her head. It was so tight and firm around her body. She looked down at herself in the odd creation. Quickly she slipped the heels on her feet and called out,

"I think I am ready Jacob!" moments later he emerged from the shadows. He paused, taken aback by his sister's speedy transformation. He took her hand and kicked the knapsack into a large bush beside them.

"Time to go then," he whispered and they were off again through the trees.

When they came out on the other side of the vast wood, Annaleise stopped in awe. The lights glistened in the distance as they looked over the high-rise jungle. Jacob had been lucky enough to experience life on the other side. This is where he had been during Rumspringa, but his freedom was short-lived. He promptly returned to the community, overwhelmed by the progression he experienced.

Annaleise had not had that luxury. This was her first time in the city, even seeing it from a distance.

"Why are you bringing me here?" she mumbled. Jacob's expression became serious.

"We need money, Annaleise. I did not want to worry you with such matters but since our parents passing we have been struggling... more than you know." she had no idea what this had to do with going to the city.

"We can get jobs here. Second jobs, at night. It has been so hard for us Annaliese and I need your help. Please," he begged. But she would do anything for her brother. She took his hand once more and squeezed it kindly.

"Then let's go," she said, excitedly.

Months later and they had been working at the diner quite regularly, almost every night. Annaleise darted around in her short, yellow waitressing uniform, serving tables left and right. After her first day, she was amazed at how much money she had made, and just in tips. In the kitchen her brother worked hastily, cleaning dish after dish and piles of cutlery. But neither of them minded the hard work, especially Annaleise. She was happy to just be out in the real world.

"Order up!" the chef boomed from the service window. He rang the bell relentlessly to alert her of food being ready to pick up. She scooted over and took it to her waiting customers. Now she had everything down to a fine art.

The sneaking around was getting quite cumbersome, however. Her heart raced each night her and Jacob ventured out, against the communities wishes. That night when she got home she collapsed on the bed and stared up at the ceiling. Exhausted, she wished her life was more simple. Leading her dual existence was taking its toll on her. She was plagued with a lack of sleep and a crippling anxiety. Tossing and turning during her few hours sleep each night. Alas, she had no other choice, for now anyway. She felt a huge debt weighing on her, for her brother. He had taken care of Annaleise since their parent's sudden demise. No matter how much she wished she could leave, it was not an option.

One morning as she was walking down the street, Annaleise was greeted by an unexpected face.

"Annaleise!" a man's voice boomed from behind her. She turned quickly on her heel to see an old friend, one whom she thought had left for good years earlier.

"Jebidiah?" she said, stunned. Her grocery basket fell to the ground with a thud as she ran toward him and wrapped her arms around his broad shoulders. He picked her up around the waist and they held their embrace for several seconds. Even though it had been so long since their last encounter, neither failed to recognize the other.

He dropped her back to the ground and she stepped back slightly to take in the sight of her long lost friend. His hair was styled just as it always had been. His dark brown locks were cut short, a few inches from his scalp. It hung in waves around his face. His skin was tanned and contrasted perfectly with his strong, masculine jawline and muscular figure. His chin was littered with stubble, giving his face a slight shadowing.

Their last meeting had not been so joyous. Jebidiah had been leaving for Rumspringa with her brother Jacob. The three children had grown up as close as they could be, spending endless hours together playing in the cornfields and chasing each other through the streets. Since the age of five, Annaleise and Jebidiah had known each other. She saw him as one of her closest friends. Or at least she had before he disappeared.

It had been a cold night, pelting down with rain. They stood there, facing each other. Annaleise had been fifteen, Jebidiah sixteen. Not a word was spoken for several minutes between them. Too young to realize the deep feelings that connected them, Jebidiah left with Jacob, to experience the modern world with the rest of the community boys coming of age that year. Annaleise had waited for him. She waited up at night and watched for him during the day. But he did not return.

Jacob came back weeks later with a few of the neighborhood boys, but Jebidiah was not among them.

Her brother had rested his hand on her shoulder as tears rolled down her face, tears for the loss of her best friend.

"He said to tell you he will see you again. He promised." at the time Annaleise had not believed him. She had thought her brother was trying desperately to bring her out of her deepening hole of overwhelming sadness. But with Jebidiah standing before her, Jacob's words echoed in the midst of her thoughts.

'He promised.'

She had given up hope of seeing him again, yet here he stood, in the flesh.

Jebidiah was speechless. He had returned to the community after years. It seemed that no matter how much the modern world drew him, his love for Annaleise was stronger. From the day he had left, he did not stop thinking about her, not for a moment. It had been fun and he savored the new experiences put forth by his peers in the city, but no one could replace her. That was what influenced him to return. There was nothing more he could gain from the city, he was looking to start a family. Jebidiah could not consider anyone else he would rather make a life with than her.

"I hope Jacob gave you my message all those years ago," he said, smiling down at her from above.

"He did," she replied, mirroring the beam that had taken over Jebidiah's face. Any onlooker could tell that these two were much more than just friends, even if they had not yet admitted it to themselves. They still grasped the hands of each other as they chatted for a few minutes about shared memories from the past.

Jebidiah bent down and picked up the discarded basket of groceries Annaleise had dropped in her shock at his appearance.

"Let's go for a walk, I need to catch up with you. So much has happened in the last few years I am sure," he laughed. As they strolled along they spoke at length about their experiences. Everything Jebidiah said about his time away absolutely intrigued her. She desperately wished that she could share in this modern world, if only for a day. Working was all she had ever had the chance to do when her and Jacob managed to escape for their night shifts.

"So, what about your life, Annaleise?" he questioned. After a moment of thought, he saw her face drop. The only significant thing she could think of to tell him was of her parent's sudden demise the previous fall. She took a deep breath and prepared herself for the retelling of the most painful memory she possessed.

"Actually, there was an accident last year," she began. Jebidiah's permanent grin faded almost immediately.

"My parents cart overturned. It was terrifying but the worst was that they did not make it." Jebidiah could not find the words to express his condolences. After a few moments to comprehend the brief and saddening story he mustered,

"I am so sorry, Annaleise."

As always, her first thought was to change the subject, and so she did. Long ago she had decided that her parents would not have wanted her to mourn, but cherish the life that she had. That was exactly what she intended to do. The sadness they had been wallowing in for that brief moment evaporated quickly as they moved on to more trivial and light-hearted news from their vast time apart.

Jebidiah walked her all the way back to her door. He handed back the basket as she stepped through the threshold of the dark, polished doorway.

"Well, I am sure we will see each other again soon," he said as he turned to leave.

"You will," she smiled and with that the door clicked shut behind her.

As the following months flew by, Annaleise found herself spending more and more of her limited free time with her long lost friend. Jebidiah found comfort in their closeness. Since moving back, he had faced endless scrutiny from the older members of the place he called home. They frowned upon him for his rash decision to leave, now that he had returned. He had known upon his abrupt return to his family that not everyone would be so welcoming. But no one else mattered as long as Annaleise was by his side.

She found comfort in his company too. She was intrigued by his endless stories of the new technologies and strange architecture he had encountered in his years away. Unlike her peers, Annaleise held nothing against him for leaving, if anything she wished that she could do the same.

The two companions spent their time just as they did, years earlier. Exploring the now familiar woods. Chasing each other through the cornfields. Collapsing with laughter on the dirt floor of the outdoors.

They savored each moment they spent in each others company. To Annaleise, no one could compare to Jebidiah.

One sunny afternoon, they fell into each other's arms in the dewy grass of the outskirts of the boundary. Their laughter subsided and Annaleise looked up at Jebidiah, beaming down at her. She knew that there was something deeper. This was not just another friendship, he meant so much more. Every second without him left her feeling cold and empty. Every second without her made him feel as if he was completely alone.

"Do you think you will stay here this time?" Annaleise asked. She hoped that his answer reflected the way that she felt. But alas, he uttered the answer she did not want to hear.

"No. I think that now I have experienced what is out there, lived my life outside the confines of the community, I don't want to leave again." her heart dropped. There was nothing in the world she wished for more than to go, but a life without Jebidiah seemed just as empty.

It was his strength that encouraged her to plan her escape, to a new life in the modern world. Deep in her heart she knew that it was unlikely Jebidiah would come with her. After all, he had returned not weeks ago, but she had to follow her dreams. She had but one life, and she intended to live it. As much as she wanted to share with him her wishes, she knew this was one secret she must keep to herself.

Jebidiah walked her home again that day, as he often did of late. The sun was setting over the sovereign hills as they strolled past people and places on the way home. She took in the sights, for in a few weeks they would be gone forever. There was no doubt she would miss this place, but most of all she would miss him. She cherished the time they had together, though short lived.

They arrived at her home. Before she opened the door, Jebidiah grasped her wrist tightly. Her skin broke out in goosebumps all over in response to his flesh against hers. Her heart raced within her chest cavity. Cheeks began to glow red as the blood from her pounding heart rushed to her face. She hoped that Jebidiah did not see the intense reaction she gave from his touch.

"Do you have plans for tomorrow?" he questioned. His expression was serious all of a sudden.

"No," Annaleise responded. Where was he going with this?

"I see, well goodnight then," he said with a grin. How strange. With that Jebidiah let go of her arm and placed his hands into his pockets.

"Goodbye," she called to him as he strolled slowly away, toward his family home at the end of the road.

As she closed the door behind her Annaleise leaned her back against the rough wood and closed her eyes. The overwhelming sensation of lust she felt for Jebidiah was quickly blooming into a raging passion. Love. Little did she know that he felt it too. From the top of her head to the far tips of her toes her entire being was filled with admiration and desire for him. How would she tell him that she was going to leave the town? Start a new life in the place that he had run from.

She already had a plan in place. Two weeks from now she would be living amongst the modern world. Jacob had not been pleased, but he knew that he could not stop his sister from following her dreams. He had the opportunity, so there was no way that he could deny her that right, regardless of the community law.

"Are you sure you will be OK on your own?" Jacob could not hide the worried tone of his voice. Not even he could brave the new world, how could his little sister live there alone?

"I will, please do not worry about me, Jacob," then she explained her plan.

In the dead of night, while the town slept, she would sneak silently through the streets. Toward the wood. The path that they had traveled hundreds of times before would lead her to her new existence. She could not leave during the day, for fear of what scrutiny she may face from the others in the town. Women rarely left and were never welcomed home. It was best for her to just disappear.

"But you have never been that way alone." he said, his voice still trembling with fear for Annaleise.

"I have mapped out our way. The last few weeks I have made a note of each landmark along the path. Each time I feel as if my feet lead me more and more. I step without hesitation." slowly she had memorized the way. Every rock and tree, branch and shrub. The dirt clearings and the overgrown mangling of tangled weeds, she was confident in her navigational ability. Even if Jacob was not so.

"Where will you stay?" his questions kept coming. But Annaleise was not one to take her decisions lightly. To his every question, she had the perfect answer. During their time at the diner, they had made a few friends, both co-workers, and customers. Annaleise had organized a room in a modest apartment with Katie, a fellow waitress at a neighboring restaurant. For only a small portion of her minimum wage, she had a place to her her own.

Several hours later, Annaleise had assured her brother that she could fend for herself. If she ever needed him, he would be there for her too.

Jacob took her hand and looked at her, eyes full of sadness.

"I will always be here for you, sister," a single tear rolled down his cheek, winding its way through the stubble on his strong chin. Annaleise was taken aback, she had not seen her brother so emotional since their parents passing. She whispered the only words that came to mind in response to his heartfelt confession.

"I know," tears now flowed freely down their faces. They sat in silence as Jacob took in the news she had revealed to him. The plan she had derived. How much he would miss her.

The hardest part was over. Annaleise had dreaded telling her brother about her escape. Now she felt free, with his blessing she could leave without hesitation. She slept that night, soundly for the first time in many moons. Dreaming of the future adventures she would have in the big city.

The next morning Jebidiah was at her door before either of the siblings had risen. She heard the light tapping from her bedroom and quickly dressed to see who was so desperate to see them this day. She raced down the creaking steps and to the front door. Opening it widely she was ecstatic to see Jebidiah standing there with a bouquet of red roses. Their scent was swept immediately into her nostrils and she closed her eyes as the aroma intoxicated her.

"Good morning, Annaleise," Jebidiah greeted her, placing the stunning bunch into her hands.

"Hello," she replied, staring at the gift he had brought for her. Something was different about him this morning. She could not pick it but his smile was strange somehow, brighter than she had seen before. His eyes sparkled in the morning light. Her heart skipped a beat as they paused for a moment, looking deeply into each other's eyes.

"I have a day planned for us," he said excitedly. Before she had time to properly lace up her boots, Jebidiah took her hand and whisked her away from her home. They walked together toward the vast cornfields at the end of the street. Waving at their fellow community members as they passed, Jebidiah led Annaleise through the tall corn stalks.

She had no idea what he had in store. They rushed forward in silence. Annaleise found her mind wandering as she took in the rays of sunlight winding through the stalks and leaves surrounding them. Her dress occasionally caught on rouge sticks and branches strewn throughout the fields. She stumbled a few times, but Jebidiah was there to catch her and help her find her feet once more.

Minutes passed and they finally arrived at the small clearing in the far end of the fields. Jebidiah let her hand drop and pulled a blanket from the backpack he had been lugging with them on the short journey. He laid it delicately out on the ground, straightening the edges and patting it down flat.

"Come, sit," he gestured to a soft spot on the blanket and she slowly approached, sitting down carefully, holding her dress flat against her thighs as she lowered her body to the ground. She watched on as Jebidiah began unpacking a picnic that he had prepared. She was stunned at the romantic setting that he had created for just the two of them, out of nowhere.

"I hope you're hungry," he laughed. Her eyes drifted from plate to plate, each piled high with sandwiches and cakes, fruit and salads. She could not believe what she saw before her. This was the kind of thing she had always dreamed of but had never eventuated into a reality. The sun beamed down on them as they began their conversations.

"Please," Jebidiah picked up a plate of her favorite sandwiches, fresh strawberry jam. She picked up one and took a bite. The sweetness of the jam found every corner of her tongue, leaving a lasting sensation in her mouth as she swallowed. He watched her intently, looking as if something was weighing heavily on his mind. Annaleise looked into his deep, brown eyes. She felt herself smile as she took in his handsome features, just inches from her. His short, dark hair flowed subtly in the mild breeze. Her gaze followed his masculine jawline and rugged chin, covered in light stubble.

It was at that moment Jebidiah uttered the words she had been longing for him to say for so long,

"I love you, Annaleise, I always have." she was taken aback. Of course, her heart reciprocated his feelings, but she could not bring herself to say the words back. In the back of her mind, she knew that if she revealed her love for him she must also let him in on the fact she was planning to leave. Leave him and everything else behind. Moments later she found her voice once more,

"I love you too."

They spoke for hours after Jebidiah's unexpected, but heartfelt, confession. Of life and the paths they wanted to take in the future. That was when troubles arose.

"I just want to settle down, and have a family. I love it so much here. It feels so right to be back." Jebidiah said in between bites of his rosy red apple. Annaleise froze. This was exactly the life she was running from. It was the first time that she realized that their journeys may lead them in different directions. She sat silent for a moment as he waited patiently for her to say something, anything. She took a deep breath and proceeded to reveal her underlying plan to Jebidiah. Her plan to leave and start a new life in the city he had fled from.

"I had no idea," Jebidiah gasped, in response to her and Jacob's secret second existence outside of the community. His heart dropped as she continued to explain her plans to escape and live amongst the modern world. Never had he thought coming into the fields with her that morning that she would drop this bombshell upon him. All hopes of his quiet life back at home with his childhood sweetheart were slowly evaporating before his eyes.

"When do you plan to leave?" he questioned, his heartbeat pounding in his chest. He prayed that it was not soon. That he would have time to change her mind.

"Two weeks from today," she admitted. His smile had faded, and hers with it. She had thought that the hardest conversation before her departure was over, but she had not counted on Jebidiah's romantic notions. His proposal of a simple, family life in the mundane town she had always lived. She loved him deeply, but her want for adventure was overwhelming.

With the sun beginning to lower over the tips of the corn, they decided that it was time to return. She folded the blanket as Jebidiah picked up the empty plates that surrounded them in the clearing. He took her hand and led the way back through the towering stalks. They moved at a much slower pace upon their return. Annaleise could not be sure, maybe it was due to the dimming light, but she felt as if their lagging pace was a bi-product of the conversations they had just had. Of her leaving him and the rest of her life behind.

Eventually, they reached her front door once more. She stepped up the front stair and peered down at him.

"Thank you for today, Jebidiah. I had an amazing time. I really appreciate all that you have done for me," Annaleise checked quickly for onlookers and before a word could escape his lips she kissed him tenderly on the cheek. By the time Jebidiah realized what had happened she had already stepped back inside.

He began his journey home, filled with mixed emotions from the day just passed. He desperately wanted Annaleise to stay, but he understood her position was difficult. With constant reminders daily of her parent's death, he could only imagine the heartache she must feel living here.

Two weeks later, the grandfather clock below the stairs began chiming midnight. Annaleise knew this was her chance to make her escape quietly, without fear of waking her sleeping neighborhood. She tiptoed down the stairs, their echoing creaks masked by the gongs of the great timekeeper. Her blonde locks fell over her face as she looked down toward the door, her destination on this dark winter night. She brushed them aside and kept moving. Grabbing the already assembled knapsack from its hiding spot, she slipped her pale pink coat over her slender shoulders and on the final stroke of midnight the door clicked shut behind her.

The cool wind bit at her exposed flesh as she crept through the dead of night. She knew that by leaving she was breaking her oath to the Church, but the call of the outside world was just too great. Not even her one true love could keep her from following her dreams. A single tear rolled slowly down her pale cheek as she looked back, back at the friends and family she would no longer see. Back at Jebidiah.

Tearing her gaze away she strove forward. Her hair was now wet with sweat, despite the cold air that stung her face and pierced her lungs. She ran, as fast as she could. Each snapping twig made her heart jump. Every sound around her made her pause for a moment. A moment was all she could spare. Slowly she kept moving, through the woods, following the hidden road to freedom. As she made her way Annaleise found her mind wandering back to all of her most cherished memories with the community and everything she was giving up. The celebrations and family dinners. Just as she lost herself completely in her thoughts a sharp noise snapped her back to reality.

She looked around desperately for somewhere to hide. She could distinguish faint footsteps coming her way. Who could be out here this late, in the cold? Annaleise was convinced that she was caught. Someone had overheard her speaking of her plan to Jebidiah, or worse he had outed her himself. She threw her knapsack into a large bush to her left and jumped behind. As she crouched on the ground crazy accusations filled her head, but she kept her blue eyes focused on the clearing before her. Was it Jebidiah who let slip her secret plan, or did someone else overhear? When a shadowy figure finally caught her eye in the woods, she waited with baited breath to identify her stalker.

Branches crunched beneath his feet as the man emerged into the grassy clearing, uncloaked by the light of the moon. Annaleise's jaw dropped and her heart raced at what felt like a thousand beats a second. She no longer needed to hide, she no longer had any fear or doubt about the path that she had chosen.

"Jebidiah!" she exclaimed, sprinting as fast as her legs could carry her toward him. A smile exploded across his face as she jumped carelessly into his outstretched arms. Jebidiah wrapped his muscular arms around her. He grasped her as tight as he could, never wanting to part again. She let her body melt into his. There they stood, nestled in each other's arms for several moments before severing their sensual embrace.

"I could not let you go, Annaleise. I love you." Jebidiah confessed. She stared into his beaming blue eyes, looking down upon her. There was only one thing that she could respond.

"I love you too," she answered. Her eyes welled up with blissful tears that soon began running, one by one, down her soft cheeks. Jebidiah reached forward and wiped them away with his calloused hands. One of her arms drew back, reaching up to run her fingers through his mess of tangled hair, damp with sweat. Still stunned by his sudden appearance, she was nothing but ecstatic to see him.

At that moment, Jebidiah leaned down and kissed her soft, cherry lips for the first time, basking in the cool blanket of moonlight penetrating the canopy. Annaleise could not believe her luck as she stood in the middle of the trees, in the arms of her love. She had been sure, not hours ago, that she had lost the love of her life forever. Now, she was on her way to making a new life for herself, in a new world, with the man of her dreams.

She leaned in closer to his warm silhouette, grasping at the fabric of his coat. She savored his touch, something she thought she had lost forever in the sands of time. His hand brushed her now flushing cheeks. He traced down her neck and over her petite shoulder. Her hand found its place against his pounding chest. And hers against his.

Jebidiah brushed a lock of hair from Annaleise's ear.

"We must go now," he whispered softly to her. Stepping back from him, she nodded in agreement. She would no longer need to start her new life alone, they were together at last. He picked up her knapsack and hauled it onto his back.

"Come," he ushered Annaleise back onto her path. Toward the city for the last time. As they neared the bustling hub, she witnessed the blanket of light illuminating the town. Never had she seen something so beautiful. Never had she felt so free.

FOREVER

UNEXPECTED

82

MONICA MARKS

Bethany felt a sharp nudge at her ribs and she quickly blinked the sleep from her eyes, startled.

"Beth, look at that!" Andrea whispered, leaning across her half-awake frame to point out the tiny window. Bethany turned her head to look out the pane and her breath caught in her throat. The plane was descending over the most breathtaking landscape which she had ever seen.

That isn't saying much, Bethany thought with dry amusement. *This is the first time I have ever been out of Indiana in my life. Still, I can't imagine that it gets much more lovely than this.*

She watched as steaming mountaintops passed beneath them and they flew above lush, green jungles as far as the eye could see.

"Attention ladies and gentlemen," a flight attendant said over the intercom. "We will be landing in Managua in fifteen minutes. Please ensure that your trays are in the upright position and your seatbelts are fastened."

Bethany checked her waist quickly for the strap and sat back against the seat. The flight had been less scary than she had anticipated. She had rather enjoyed the journey through the clouds.

It's a little bit like being next to God, Bethany thought. She cast a sidelong look at Andrea who was still straining over her lap to take in the scenery.

She is so excited about this trip. I wonder why she does these missions so often. You would think she would be discouraged by the futility behind them. No matter how many supplies we send or hours we volunteer, the locals continued to be sick but the thousands. It's like ramming your head against a wall.

For Bethany's part, she had been basically blackmailed into joining the church group on that excursion. Pastor Frank had pulled her aside one afternoon after choir practice.

"Your voice has become more lovely with each passing year, Bethany," he told her appreciatively. "We are so blessed to have you in our choir."

"Thank you, Pastor," she replied, smiling demurely. She was pleased by the young Reverend's compliment. Like the other young ladies in the parish, she had somewhat of a school girl's crush on James Frank. He was still unmarried and there was a playful competition among the women to see who might be able to win his affections. Yet as the years melted by, it became apparent that Pastor Frank had no mind for marriage, at least not to any of the single women in his midst. Still, Bethany could not help but feel flattered by his kind words.

"Bethany, I wanted to ask you about something," Pastor Frank continued and Bethany turned her green eyes to stare up at him.

"Sure," she replied. "Ask away."

Pastor Frank cleared his throat and looked uncomfortably at his shoes. Bethany was immediately filled with a sense of caution.

Uh oh...is he speaking on behalf of my parents?

"We have a mission upcoming to Nicaragua," he said slowly, maintaining his gaze on the floor. Bethany was already shaking her dark hair. Every time a trip was planned to some God forsaken third world environment, he tried to recruit her. Bethany could think of nothing less appealing than spending two weeks in a suffocating country, encased in flies. It was not that Bethany was heartless. She volunteered at the church's soup kitchen every second weekend and worked as a camp counsellor with the developmentally challenged in the summer. Bethany was thrilled to help in any way she could; at home.

"Before you refuse, Bethany, I should tell you that we will be forced to cancel the trip if we don't find one more body. You have never gone on a mission, have you?"

"No, I haven't," Bethany agreed. "And I have no interest in going now."

Pastor Frank shook his head sadly.

"I know how you feel about these excursions, Bethany but I wouldn't be asking if you weren't my only hope."

Bethany gritted her teeth and stared at her hands. She knew that Jeanie Williams would typically be the sixth person to go but she had just had a baby. She wracked her brain for anyone else to replace Jeanie but she was coming up blank. She imagined that Pastor Frank had already done the same.

"I wouldn't be asking you if we had another option, Beth," Pastor Frank assured her. "I promise you, this will be a life changing experience for you. When you see the children's faces light up, it will all be worth it."

If I say no, they will cancel the trip and everyone will be angry at me, Bethany thought miserably. *There really isn't much of a choice, is there?*

Bethany sighed heavily.

"When do we leave?"

As the aircraft descended into the surreal beauty of Managua, Bethany could not help but feel a spark of excitement.

"I hope Dr. Martinez is still here," Andrea breathed as the landing gear touched the runway. "In all the missions I have ever done, he is the best doctor I have ever seen. The children love him and he is so caring."

Bethany rolled her eyes.

"He's a doctor, Andy. That's basically in his job description," she replied.

Andrea's eyes clouded over as she shook her head.

"You would think so," Andrea answered sadly. "But the stress of the job gets to most of them. The death and sickness turns what were probably great doctors into robots. I have been to countries where they treat their patients like an assembly line. One physician in Liberia actually would scream, 'next!' and shove the patient off the bed to make room for another. It was horrifying." Bethany was shocked but she was certain Andrea was exaggerating. Doctors were well paid for their roles. Why else would someone become a doctor?

"Ladies and gentleman, we have arrived in Managua, Nicaragua. The temperature here is a balmy 101 degrees and the sun is shining. We hope you had a pleasant flight aboard American Airlines flight 867 and we thank you for flying with us. Have a lovely stay in Nicaragua."

One hundred and one degrees? What kind of hell on earth have we flown into? Bethany thought woefully. Her mood was already souring at the thought of the heat.

Slowly, seatbelts came off and Andrea rose into the aisle to allow for Bethany to follow her onto the runway tarmac. The women blinked at the intense rays of sun as they descended the stairs. Bethany's legs were cramped from the four-hour flight and she realized she was thirsty.

"Do you have any water," she asked Andrea as they walked into the Augusto C. Sandino International Airport. Andrea nodded and dug a bottle from inside her carryon bag. Bethany took a swig and wiped her brow. She was already sweating.

They walked toward the luggage carousel to wait for their bags. The rest of their group had arrived the previous day with the supplies. Andrea and Bethany had been unable to get on that flight which was fine with Bethany. It just meant one less day that she would be stuck in Central America.

"Oh, there's one of yours, Beth," Andrea told her, gesturing at the bags. Instantly, a young boy appeared at her side. Bethany guessed him to be no older than eight. He was filthy and wore a flimsy, holey t-shirt. His knees were scarred and thin in a pair of shorts that were swimming trunks and much too large for his small form. His flip flops were as good as bare feet, they had eroded so badly. He offered Bethany and Andrea a bright smile.

"I help!" he declared, rushing to grab the bag.

"No, wait!" Bethany yelled but Andrea put her hand on her companion's arm and shook her head.

"Just let him get it," she whispered. "He's only looking to make a dollar."

Bethany was alarmed as she watched the frail boy struggle with the luggage. She rushed over to assist him with wrestling the bag over the belt. Panting, the child waved her away.

"I have," he told her. "More?"

Swallowing, Bethany nodded and pointed out their other belongings. The child refused any more help, almost knocking himself over with the heavy items.

He is too small to be doing this, she thought, but she did not interfere. She glanced at Andrea and she could see the compassion in the older woman's face.

When they had claimed their belongings, the boy piled up the mound and rolled behind them, still beaming happily. Bethany desperately wanted to sent the boy on his way but Andrea seemed content having him assist.

They cleared customs and exited the gate, the boy faithfully at their side.

"How long is he going to carry our bags?" Bethany finally whispered to Andrea, her heart breaking.

"Until they are loaded into a car safely," she replied calmly but Bethany could see she was as affected by the child's struggling as she.

Bethany clamped her mouth closed.

She has more experience in these things than I do but still…

"Andrea!" A tall, intelligent looking man was hurrying toward them, the beam on his tired face lighting the dusty airport. Andrea squealed in a childlike fashion, causing Bethany to give her a strange look. She had never seen her friend look so excited. The man approached and embraced Andrea warmly. He stepped back and Bethany examined him furtively.

Ah, this is probably the doctor she was talking about on the plane, Bethany thought, eyeing the handsome man. He wore thin green scrubs which were worn with age but it brought out the warm glow of his bronze skin and wavy black hair. His eyes were wide and cat-shaped with extremely long lashes, framing a set of intense, brown eyes. He was taller than Bethany expected, towering over both the women but at least six inches.

"Dr. Martinez, this is Bethany Grieger. This is her first mission anywhere so you will have to show her some extra attention," Andrea joked. The doctor rested his eyes on Bethany, his eyes lighting up as he stared at her expressive jade eyes.

"Welcome to Managua, Betany," he said cordially, offering her a long hand. "I hope this will not be your last trip with us."

Bethany accepted it, relishing his lilting accent and his inability to pronounce the "h" in her name.

"Nice to meet you, Dr. Martinez," she told him. Their gazes locked for a moment and time seemed to slow momentarily. He broke the spell, turning his attention the boy with the luggage.

"I see you have met Dario," he said, ruffling the child's hair. Dario smiled up at the doctor.

"Hola, doctor," Dario smiled. The two exchanged a few words in Spanish before Dr. Martinez gestured for the women to follow them

"Excuse me for speaking in our native tongue," he told them apologetically. "Dario's sister has been very sick and I wanted to know how she was doing. Unfortunately, his English is not fluent."

"What is wrong with his sister?" Bethany asked as they made their way back into the sunshine.

"She is suffering from cholera," Dr. Martinez answered sadly and Bethany gasped.

"Oh, how awful! How old is she?"

Dario began to load the bags into a beat-up VW bus, his smile never wavering.

"She is five but luckily she is on the upswing," Dr. Martinez replied. Dario finished heaving the luggage into the back of the van and turned to the group. Andrea already had a bill in her hand which she deposited into Dario's small palm. The boy looked at the crumpled paper in his hand, his mouth dropping open.

"Oh, gracias, senora! Muchas gracias!" he almost sobbed, clutching the money. His dark eyes were filled with grateful tears and he scampered off as if he was worried Andrea was going to change her mind.

"How much did you give him?" Bethany asked as they jumped into the vehicle.

"I only gave him five dollars but that's as good as a hundred-dollar bill around here," she murmured back. Again, Bethany was overcome with sadness.

Dr. Martinez took the wheel and began to drive out of the airport area. Bethany marveled at how laid back the travellers seemed. It was contrary to anything she had ever seen in the United States. No one seemed to be in a rush to go anywhere. As if reading her thoughts, Dr. Martinez spoke.

"Our way of life is quite a bit different than that you are accustomed," he told her. "Nicaragua is the second poorest country in the western hemisphere. Our major exports are coffee, tobacco, sugar and gold but of course those products are very weather and climate dependant. Tourism has increased in the past decade so we are told our economy is on the rise however, there is still much disease and a need for clean water."

Bethany leaned forward between the front seats to absorb every word.

"I thought that there were many fresh water lakes in this country," Bethany piped up and Dr. Martinez nodded.

"That is true but they are mostly infested with bacteria. We simply don't have the resources to filter the water. Most people drink from the lakes and end up with E-coli, parasites and in the case of Dario's sister, Luz, cholera."

Bethany was aghast.

"We have to do something about that!" she cried passionately and both Andrea and the doctor chuckled gently.

"There simply is not the money," he said sadly. "But God sends us angels like you to make things easier sometimes."

They were silent for the remainder of the trip, Bethany lost in thought as the lush but impoverished setting slipped before her wide eyes.

They don't have clean water and they get sick from it. If they don't have money for clean water, they definitely don't have money for the medicine to cure them of the illnesses. It makes more sense for them to spend the money on the water than it does to pay for the aftermath of drinking tainted liquid. But if there is no money, how do we make this happen?

Bethany had no answer.

When they arrived at their hotel, Bethany was immediately repulsed. The three-story building was crumbling from the inside out. Their room was miniscule and stifling hot.

"Where is the bathroom?" she asked Andrea, dropping her case reluctantly onto the floor beside one of the twin beds.

"It's a common bathroom down the hall," she replied, plopping heavily onto the bed. A huge insect scurried out from its hiding spot, causing Bethany to scream. Andrea laughed.

"You better get used to the bugs," she teased. "There are creatures you can't imagine in these parts. And lizards as big as your head."

Bethany shuddered, eyeing the scuttling insect. She closed her eyes and took a deep breath.

I can do this for thirteen more days, she told herself. *Just focus on the sick kids and forget about the twenty-six-legged animal under your bed.*

Bethany was sure she wouldn't sleep for the remainder of the trip.

"Get changed. We have to get to the clinic," Andrea pressed. "We have to meet the others soon."

Bethany nodded and headed into the hallway to find the washroom. The plumbing was ancient and everything leaked from the sink to the toilet. The shower consisted of a drain over a set of floor tiles and a long hose.

I wonder if this water is safe for showering.

She wet a washcloth and wiped her face carefully, avoiding her orifices lest the water was contaminated. She would have to ask Andrea about it.

Or I can ask the doctor, Bethany thought, her mind recalling the wisdom and depth of his brown eyes. *I bet he knows everything.*

Bethany returned to the room and slipped into a simple white sundress.

"What do we do at the clinic?" she asked, waiting for Andrea to get ready.

"We will devise a plan. Half of us will go to the church for the first week and supply the children with books, pencils, papers and other necessities for school. We'll do activities with the kids, just as we do at home in Sunday school. The second week, we will switch and stay at the clinic helping the doctors with the sick. Dr. Martinez will show you what needs to be done there. We'll figure out which group you and I will fall into when we meet the others today."

Bethany was surprised to find herself hoping she was on clinic duty.

I am interested to see how medicine is handled in the third world, she told herself but she knew she was lying. She wanted to spend more time with the attractive doctor. She had only spent moments with Dr. Martinez but she found him intriguing. His work was thankless and never ending yet he maintained an almost cheerful aura as if he was unaffected by the endless suffering in which he was surrounded.

Andrea turned to her and waved a chubby hand.

"I'm ready, Beth. Let's go – the car will be waiting."

When they arrived at the Managua Children's Clinic, Bethany was taken aback. The air of serenity which had floated over Managua, shadowing them from the airport had evaporated. In its place was havoc. In every corner of the tiny building lay children in various stages of agony. Some were vomiting on the floor, others were clinging to their defeated looking mothers. The stench of disease and urine wafted into her nose but Bethany was too wrapped up in the mollifying sights to notice the putrid stench. While a few small beings were lucky enough to have claimed beds, the majority were laying on the floor. Almost all of them were crying. Bethany fought back her own tears, springing into action.

"What can I do?" she cried to Andrea. To her surprise, the older woman stood back, her mouth turned down in grief.

"Just wait. The doctor will tell us what to do," she replied but Bethany could barely hear her above the din.

"We just can't stand here!" Bethany insisted. "We have to do something!"

Andrea shook her head and her shoulders sagged.

"It is always like this," she replied, anguish in her voice. "All we can do is wait for Dr. Martinez to tell us what to do or else we may be more of a hindrance than a help."

As if on cue, the doctor hurried up to them.

"Ah wonderful! You have arrived. How is your hotel?" Bethany stared at him in disbelief.

How can he ask about our hotel when these children are in such pain?

But as she had the thought, she quickly realized he was simply trying to put them at ease.

"Fine," she replied shortly. "What can I do here?"

Nodding approvingly at her eagerness to get started, he handed her a pair of scrubs and another pair to Andrea.

"After you have put these on, go around to all of the children and try to have them drink a few sips of water. Do not give them too much or they will vomit and it will not only be counterproductive, it will be a waste of good water. There are cases of bottled water which your group brought in my office yesterday. I have the key and you will need to come to me for it every time you need more bottles. I have the only copy. It is important that you keep whatever bottles you have on you at all times or they will be stolen."

Bethany stared at him in shock.

"Who will steal bottles of water from sick children?" she choked in disbelief. Dr. Martinez shrugged as if the information was commonplace.

"These are desperate times, Betany. The children you see here are merely the tip of the iceberg. There are many who live too far away to come here for medical attention. Their families are just as desperate to see them well as the families you see here."

Bethany paled, thinking of impoverished children laying untreated in remote areas of the country, waiting for certain death.

"What happens to them? They are just left to die?" Bethany demanded, gulping at the thought. Dr. Martinez shook his head and smiled.

"No, of course not. I will go to the rural areas three times a week after I leave the clinic to tend to those children also. Luz, Dario's sister is one of my out patients. If I get word of a sick child, I attend to them right away but oftentimes, I am not notified until it is much too late."

Bethany was overcome with emotions so strong, she was almost brought to her knees.

When does this man sleep? He works all day and then travels around at night to do the same, horrific work.

He seemed to read her mournful expression and offered her another kind smile.

"Sometimes they get well," he told her, handing her the key. "We must focus on the positive because that is all we have." She nodded and snapped to attention, hurrying toward the office. She threw on the scrubs and armed herself with several bottles of water which she found piled in a corner.

There are not nearly enough bottles here, she thought, looking hopelessly at the cases. She returned to the exterior of the clinic and knelt next to the nearest child.

"Hi, honey," she whispered to the little girl of about two. The child stared up at her with hollow, hurting eyes and Bethany fought the urge to sob.

"Have some water," she offered, pressing the bottle to her parched lips. The baby tried to struggle against her but Bethany held her firmly and managed to get a few drops of water into her.

"Rest now," she whispered, stroking her tiny face. As if she understood, her lids closed heavily. Bethany moved on to the next child and, sweetly feeding him the clean liquid.

Bethany had been at it for over an hour, oblivious to everything but the little bodies in her care when someone tapped her shoulder. Slightly annoyed at the distraction, Bethany peered up and found herself staring into Dr. Martinez's deep eyes. Her irritation dissolving, she rose to her feet.

"I'm sorry to interrupt you, Miss Betany," he told her, his thick Spanish accent still unable to handle the "h" in her name. "But you forgot to return the key to me."

Apologetically, Bethany reached into the small pocket in her scrubs to retrieve the office key.

"I'm sorry," she told him, handing it back to him. "I am just on my way over there now anyway. I need more water."

Dr. Martinez looked around appreciatively.

"You managed to get a lot of them to drink," he remarked. "That is no easy feat. Most are feeling so ill, they will not accept anything orally."

Bethany lowered her head humbly.

"They did not fuss very much," she told him. "I fear they are too sick to argue."

The two turned back to the office and Dr. Martinez unlocked the door to allow them to enter.

"Dr. Martinez – "

He faced her abruptly.

"Please call me Jasiel," he told her. Bethany felt a small fission of pleasure course through her as he said his name. His fixed his penetrating eyes upon her and she felt her cheeks stain pink under his gaze.

"Jasiel," she continued, trying to force the blush from her cheeks. "Where do you get aid from if things are so dire in your country?"

He pursed his lips together as he dug through the drawers looking for something.

"Mostly we depend on emergency relief from other countries. The United States in a big provider in assistance. The biggest problem we face, unfortunately, is that we simply do not have enough medical staff to deal with the sick."

Bethany busied herself collecting more bottles, her mind racing with thoughts.

We will have to do something about this.

The week seemed to fly by, the days blurring together one after the other. There was no time to explore the ancient and mystic city of Managua as the group worked tirelessly from sun up to sun down at the clinic. Even though she was in the company of her fellow church friends, Bethany barely saw them except briefly in the mornings and evenings at meals. When they finally made it back to the hotel, they inhaled supper and generally fell into a deep, exhaustive slumber. Bethany's concern that she would be unable to sleep with the critters with whom she was rooming proved unfruitful. The lizards had begun to grow on her with their nonchalant expressions and beady little eyes.

The only constant that Bethany had was Jasiel who seemed to take special interest in helping her adjust. He allowed her to perform basic medical procedures, despite her protests.

"I have no training!" she had cried the first time he handed her a needle. The handsome doctor had shaken his head wryly, pressing the instrument into her hand.

"Then you are still more qualified than most of the people whom we have here," he replied. Gulping, Bethany had accepted and under his careful guidance, she began administering much needed medicine to the children.

On the fourth day, little Lilliam rose to her feet and walked for the first time. She had been in the clinic for two weeks, unable to move.

"Jasiel!" Bethany screeched. "Lilliam is walking!"

He had nodded stoically but his face registered relief.

"Thank God," he whispered. "I was beginning to lose faith in her chances for survival."

Bethany impulsively embraced him in a hug before attending to the child. She did not see the look of longing gave to her disappearing back.

Later that evening as they began to close the clinic, Jasiel took her aside and out of earshot of Andrea and Jack who were stripping the linens from the beds.

"It was because of you that Lilliam finally was able to move from bed," he told her solemnly. Pleased but unwilling to take the credit, Bethany shook her head.

"No, it was God's hand at work here," she told him.

"Yes, it was God who sent you to us but it was your attention to that child which made her well again. If we had only a few more people to spend the time with these babies..."

Bethany did not know how to respond. She looked into his eyes, wanting desperately to end his suffering as much as he wished to end that of the children. He gave her a weak smile and again, Bethany was affected by a shiver.

Over and above his tireless efforts, he must be very lonely. He spends most of his time alone or surrounded by children. I wonder how his wife feels about him being gone so often.

Bethany decided to ask.

"How does your wife handle your hours?" she blurted out. He raised an eyebrow in surprise.

"I am not married. No woman in her sane mind would stand for the type of work I have committed myself to." He paused and looked at Bethany thoughtfully. "I thought you would have figured out that I was unmarried by now."

A rush of heat colored Bethany's cheeks under his wistful stare. She dropped her head in embarrassment.

He feels it too, she thought, her heart pounding in her chest. *We have a connection but it can never be...can it?*

"Beth! Dr. Martinez is here!" Andrea called from the doorway later that evening. Bethany almost tripped over her feet in her rush to the threshold. Andrea tried to step out of her way but the size of the room made the dance almost impossible. Eventually, Andrea ended up behind the flimsy wooden door. Jasiel stood in the hallway appearing exhausted.

"Jasiel, what are you doing here?" she asked, shooting Andrea a covert glance. The woman raised her eyebrow questioningly.

"Jasiel?" she mouthed silently, trapped in her spot but Bethany ignored her.

"I hope you will forgive the intrusion, Betany," he said. "But I am about to head into the rural areas. I thought you might wish to join me and meet some of the children outside of the city."

Eagerly, Bethany nodded. She had been wondering about the children outside the city. Her plan had been to ask to accompany him later in the week but it seemed that he had read her mind.

"I would love to!" she exclaimed and Jasiel nodded happily. "I'll be back later, Andy."

Andrea shrugged her shoulders and collapsed on the bed.

"I'll likely be sound asleep," she replied, already closing her eyes.

The drive from Managua to Masaya took forty-five minutes in Jasiel's old van and it was the first time Bethany had an opportunity to see the incredible Nicaraguan countryside. Bethany's breath was stolen by the towering palms and the untouched landscape.

"This is what the dinosaurs saw!" Bethany proclaimed, staring open-mouthed at the mountains against the glorious sunset. Jasiel chuckled.

"Yes, we do not have much industry in Nicaragua," he agreed.

As night began to fall, the smooth fields became a sprinkling of dilapidated shanties and Jasiel pulled his car to a stop. A sudden fear seized Bethany as people began to poke their heads from the depth of the seemingly abandoned properties.

"There are people in there," she whispered as Jasiel collected supplies. He glanced at her, realizing she was serious.

"Yes, Betany. This is where people live," he told her.

Just when I thought I could not be any more shocked by the living conditions in this country, Bethany thought, gritting her teeth. She quickly began to assist the doctor and followed him up to a tin shack. Immediately, the door flew open and Dario stood, his eyes red from crying. He began to babble in Spanish and was joined by an older woman. The two barraged Jasiel with words which Bethany could not understand but she recognized the urgency in their tone.

"What happened?" she whispered, almost running after Jasiel into the house. He did not need to answer. Laying on a pallet on the floor was a small girl in the throes of eternal sleep. A hand flew to Bethany's mouth as she gasped back a sob. It was Dario's sister, Luz.

The doctor leaned forward to check for signs of life but there were none. Luz was gone.

Bethany wanted to scream, to cry out and yell at God but she did none of those things. This was not about her deep regret. Dario and his mother had lost a small, precious soul and their anguish was fresh and real. Immediately, Bethany reached out to embrace Dario who clung to her like a burr. She whispered calmingly into his ear as he cried, his frail body trembling in shock.

Jasiel scooped up Luz's lifeless body and walked her to the van while Bethany stroked Dario's hair. When he returned, he spoke to the family in low tones and nodded at Bethany to follow him.

"We must return to Managua to arrange for Luz's body to be cremated," Jasiel told her. "The family has no means to provide for a proper burial."

His voice was raw with grief. Bethany slowly reclaimed her seat on the passenger's side of the car and lowered her gaze so she would not see Luz's mother chasing after the van, calling out for her daughter.

On the sixth day, it was time for the group to switch. Bethany was supposed to join Andrea and Jack at the church but as she reluctantly geared up for the switch that morning at the hotel, there was a knock at the door.

Aimee Thompson, the mission co-ordinator wanted to speak with Bethany.

"There's been a change of plans if it's okay with you," Aimee told her. Bethany stared at her quizzically.

"Dr. Martinez has requested that you stay at the clinic for the remainder of the trip. He says that the children have become very attached to you and honestly, it's not fair to upset them any more than they've already been upset. Is that something you can live with?" Aimee asked. Bethany nodded with too much enthusiasm.

"Oh, yes ma'am!" she declared. "I can definitely stay at the clinic for the rest of the trip!"

As Aimee left, Andrea shot Bethany a sly smile.

"I'm sure it's only for the good of the children," Andrea joked. "It has nothing to do with the handsome, attentive doctor who seems to stare at you everywhere you go."

"Of course it's for the children!" Bethany retorted angrily. "What a horrible suggestion that I am using sick kids for a romantic interest."

Andrea lost the smile and shook her head.

"I would never say that. I know your heart and intentions are true, Beth. I would also have to be deaf, blind and dumb not to see the way you and Dr. Martinez have connected...or can I call him Jasiel also?"

Bethany grimaced. Luz's death had a much bigger impact on her than she had expected, affecting her mood substantially. She had thrown herself completely into the care of the children, staying well after the others had gone back to the hotel for the night. She and Jasiel had become joined at the hip and while Luz had been the one that got away, other boys and girls seemed to be thriving in the short time since she had arrived.

"Well, I hope you don't become too attached, Beth. You're going to be heartbroken when it's time to go home," Andrea commented casually. Bethany felt the blood drain from her face. She had purposely avoided thinking about the impending departure but Andrea's words had forced the unwanted thoughts into mind.

What will I do when it is time to leave?

On the last night the group was to be in Nicaragua, Jasiel appeared at the hotel again. This time Bethany answered the door. Her heart was an explosion of bittersweet emotion as she stared into his soulful eyes.

"Would do you do me the honor of having dinner with me this evening?" he asked her. Not trusting her voice, Bethany nodded and allowed for Jasiel to lead her into the city. He had arranged for a romantic table inside a small, cozy restaurant.

As soon as they were seated, he grasped her hands.

"Betany, I want you to know that these last two weeks have been the best since I began my medical career. I have never been so in tune with anyone or met another person who seemed to care about the children as much as I do."

Bethany forced a lump down her windpipe and willed herself not to cry.

"I know we are worlds apart but I wanted to let you know how I feel before you leave. I hope you will consider coming back on another trip."

Bethany blinked the tears from her eyes.

"What has happened here has exceeded my wildest imagination," she told him seriously, squeezing his palms. "I have never felt more enlightened or awake..."

Or in love, she added silently. They shared a melancholic smile and forced themselves to concentrate on their last moments together, pushing the impending unhappiness of tomorrow from their minds.

"That was a lovely trip," Andrea commented, as the plane began to taxi down the runway. She nodded absently, staring toward the airport.

"I think that we are making some progress here, though, don't you?" Andrea asked. Her question went unanswered and she sighed heavily.

"Hello? Are you ignoring me for any particular reason?"

She turned to face Andrea and smiled sheepishly.

"Sorry. I am just wondering if we made the right decision allowing Bethany to stay behind," Aimee replied. Andrea laughed.

"I don't think we had much of a choice," Andrea replied. "Short of dragging her on the plane, she was staying."

Aimee nodded absently, a sweet smile touching her lips. She raised her eyes toward the ceiling of the aircraft and winked.

"You know what you're doing up there," she told the heavens.

A RUSH OF GRACE

MONICA MARKS

Melissa

The weather seemed to mimic her sentiments as the rain splattered relentlessly down her shirt and slithered through her pant legs, to her shoes, creating a sloshing puddle in the base of the worn soles. Well, the holes don't seem like such a big deal now, do they? She thought to herself, bemused. She tried to adjust the umbrella but there was no angle that the wind wasn't sending the rain so the effort was an exercise in futility. She cocked her head to the side and peered down the street again to see if the bus was approaching but she could not see much through the spattering on her cheeks. Sighing she retreated into the already crammed bus shelter. The bus was late and that was nothing new but the grumbling within the glass enclosure was almost too much for Melissa to bear in her current state. She almost went back out to stand in the storm to avoid listening to the commuters irritated complaints. Every day after work it was the same twenty people making the same inane conversations about the weather and politics and how the bus was inevitably late. Usually Melissa welcomed the idle chatter as a distraction to her own woes but today she was overwhelmed with depression. She reached into her enormous handbag and retrieved her cell phone. She peered at it hopefully but of course it was still out of service. The bill hadn't been paid in three months. It was probably for the best – Michelle's divorce was about to be finalized and Melissa wasn't sure she had the internal strength to listen to any more of her sister's tears. She was immediately ashamed by her thought. Michelle was having a terrible time. This marriage had only lasted six months. Melissa didn't understand how Michelle kept tying the knot when her unions always seemed to fail so miserably. Some people just can't be alone. I hope I am not one of those people. Dear God, please let mine and Greg's marriage last forever. Again, she was flooded with guilt. Of course, they would last forever. They had been together since infancy, grown up together two houses apart. Greg had adored her for as long as she could remember and she, him. Yet Melissa couldn't help but feel that there had been a shadow cast upon them since their engagement last spring. Almost as soon as he had proposed, things had gone from bad to worse. Melissa's mother had been diagnosed with terminal breast cancer and died three months later. Melissa's biological father had appeared after a ten-year absence but only because he thought he could somehow capitalize on her mother's passing. When that didn't pan out for him, he skipped town once more. Michelle had just finalized her second divorce at that time. Then Greg lost his job at the factory and was picking up odd jobs wherever he could find them. The only constant had been Melissa. Melissa and her meager paying waitressing gig at the truck stop. She managed to keep paying the property taxes on the house after her mom went to heaven and she helped maintain the payments on Greg's truck so he could still go job hunting and work jobs when he got them but money was beyond tight and the wedding date was approaching faster than she had anticipated. *I should ask Greg about changing the date.* But some little nagging voice in her head told her if she did that, the date would never occur at all. Before she could chastise her subconscious for such an appalling notion, the bus flew up unexpectedly, drenching her further. Sighing, she boarded the bus, swishing, and squeaking. The vehicle was filled to capacity and Melissa was standing wedged between an old Asian man who smelled quite like a summer meadow and a seated middle-aged woman. She looked apologetically at the woman as droplets of water dripped off her shabby coat and onto the lady. The woman looked up at Melissa with luminous gray eyes and smiled in a way that actually warmed her right to the core of her heavy heart. For one brief second, Melissa felt content. Then a confusion set it.

"I'm sorry, ma'am. The rain..." Melissa trailed off. The woman continued to smile at her but said nothing. She merely shook her head and shrugged. Melissa was overcome by a strange sense of de ja vu.

"Ma'am, do I know you?" she asked timidly. It always sounded so cliché when people asked that question. The lady's smile widened but she shook her head again.

"I don't think so, child," she replied. Her voice was a light, throaty whisper. "But God bless you." Then she stood up but before she shuffled away toward the exit, she reached up, touched the gold cross which hung around her neck and stroked Melissa's cheek. The chain and pendant had belonged to her mother.

"Remember, child, the darkest hour is just before the dawn." And then she was gone.

Melissa literally had to wring out her clothes once she walked into the safety of her house. The storm seemed to have worsened over the hour and a half it had taken her to get home. She was freezing and sniffling and just before she could jump into the welcoming warmth of the newly filled bathtub, the doorbell rang. For a brief moment, looking at the almost steaming water in her peripheral vision, she contemplated ignoring the caller but she was fairly certain it was either Greg or Michelle. With that realization, the urge to ignore grew stronger. Alas, Melissa was not the girl to turn her back on her family; no matter how much they deserved it.

She threw on a pair of pajamas and hurried down the rickety stairs to the front door. Greg pushed his way into the house, already soaked to his skin.

"Sorry," he apologized as he rushed for shelter, pooling water all over the fading carpet. "That storm is really something else!"

Melissa nodded her agreement and after shutting the door joined her fiancé in the living room.

"I would have called you today but my phone got cut off," she told him after giving him a brief hug and kiss. Greg looked guiltily at the floor.

"I know. I tried calling you too. I'm so sorry about that, Mel. Things will turn around soon. I worked today on a construction crew and they seemed to like me. I'm going back tomorrow too."

"Tomorrow? We're supposed to go looking for wedding venues tomorrow. It's my only day off this week, Greg."

"I know, Mel but we need the money. Listen, I was thinking about something..." Melissa looked at him expectantly. Then she shook her head when she saw the look in his eye. She already knew what he was going to say. This was probably the biggest problem with their relationship; even their thoughts were not sacred because they had known each other for so long a time.

"No. We've talked about this and the answer is still no, Greg."

"Oh come on, Mel. I can barely afford my car and you certainly can't afford this place by yourself. We should move in together and save some money for the wedding."

"No. This is my mom's house and she wouldn't have wanted us living together in it before we were married. No. End of discussion." Greg grunted and threw his hands up.

"Well at this rate, we're going to have to elope then." Melissa glared at him. He knew how important this wedding was to her. Everyone in her family had either eloped, divorced or gotten married at City Hall. There had not been one real ceremony in her immediate family, even with Michelle's three unions. Melissa desperately wanted to start her life with her husband properly, building a solid foundation from the get-go. Suddenly, she had an appalling thought. Maybe he's not the husband I'm supposed to build with.

Irene

I should have stayed home and taken that bath I never got, Melissa thought with some bitterness as she pushed her way through the marketplace. The rain had slowed to a miserable drizzle now, the sky lighter but still as gray and glum as Melissa was feeling. She didn't know what was wrong with her lately. It was so unlike her to be in such a grumpy place emotionally but she simply couldn't seem to shake the sense of doom which was stalking her. That morning when she had woken, she was determined to make the most of her day off so she forced a smile on her face and headed outside to face the world. And slowly, the rain and the late bus and the crowds chipped away at that fake beam until she was in the middle of the market, sulking again. She made her way into the center of the hub, not really sure what she was doing there. There were flowers to be bought, a band to be booked, food to be arranged but Melissa had only been thinking of the dress. Money had been so tight, she had taken to rummaging through her closet, looking for pieces of clothing she could possibly fashion into a wedding gown. Her mother's beautiful lace and satin piece had been horribly water damaged in the flood of '97 and Melissa had cried when she removed it, decaying from a trunk in the attic. Her dream had always been to wear it walking down the aisle with her father. She had a daydream where her father would turn to her on that magical day, look her in the eye and whisper, "You look just like your mother." But now that dream was shattered too. Who was she kidding? Her dad wouldn't walk her down the aisle unless she paid him. Ten years prior, he had made a startling announcement to his wife, Melissa's mother. He had fallen in love with Aunt Cathleen and they were moving to Mexico. No one had been more stunned than Melissa by the news. She had always idolized her father and her mother's sister had always been her favorite aunt. Now, in one fell swoop, both of them were gone. And gone they were. No one heard a word from them until four years later, when he called drunk, single and begging his daughters for money. Aunt Cathleen had left him for a much younger man and thrown him out of their houseboat in Mexico. Of course, neither Michelle nor Melissa were in a place to help him financially but somehow, the siblings had managed to procure a loan through a ridiculously high-interest rate through an independent company and gave him five thousand dollars. He vowed "to the good Lord Jesus above" that he would make every payment but by the time the first installment was due, his phone had been disconnected and no one heard from him again until their mother had passed. Michelle had put the loan on her bankruptcy but Melissa's credit was still ruined from her end. Yet it wasn't the money that scarred them. It was the betrayal by a man they had once loved so dearly.

Melissa angrily brushed a tear away from her face and suddenly stopped to look around. She was in an unfamiliar part of the market. This must be new. I've never seen this side before. As she looked over her shoulder, trying to orient herself, she heard a weak voice to her left.

"Are you lost, child?" Melissa turned to address the speaker. An ancient figure sat in a scarce booth, peering at her intently with large, inquisitive eyes. Melissa shook her head at the elderly woman and tried to smile but failed terribly. Suddenly, she felt overwhelmed by grief and loss. The woman was at her side in a nimble fashion one would not expect from someone so old. She patted her shoulder comfortingly.

"Come sit with me, child," the woman murmured, leading her behind the booth. "Why don't you tell me about it. I always find when I speak my worries aloud, they don't seem so cumbersome." Melissa swallowed the lump in her throat and sat on a wooden stool with the woman. She forced a small grin through her misty eyes.

"I'm sorry, ma'am. I...I'm supposed to be getting married soon...and I just don't know if I'm ready." Melissa's smiled broadened as she heard the lameness of her words but the lady just nodded sympathetically. Her shining green eyes shifted to the gold cross around Melissa's neck and she leaned forward, gently touching Melissa's golden crown of hair with a gnarled, arthritic hand.

"Have you a dress yet?"

Without warning, Melissa burst into a sea of tears as she shook her head.

"I can't afford a dress!" she moaned. "I can barely afford to eat! I don't know how we're going to have a wedding! I don't know if I should even be marrying him. Oh!"

Mortified, she jumped to her feet. "I am so terribly sorry! I don't know what came over me!"

The woman calmly placed her hands on Melissa's shoulders and sat her down on the stool again.

"You needed to get it out, child. An old woman's ears are the best place to do such things. Sometimes we even have solutions." For the first time, the old woman smiled and it was a gruesome sight. She was missing all but two of her teeth, one in the far bottom and one in the top front. Melissa cringed slightly and was instantly contrite. This person was showing her kindness in a time when she felt so incredibly alone.

When she was confident Melissa was not about to move again, the old timer shuffled to the side and Melissa was staring at an absolutely stunning wedding gown on a hanger. It was reminiscent of another era but which one, Melissa could not pinpoint. It had all of the elegance of the early 1920s with the flair of the 30's and 40's. It was a compilation of lace, crinoline and satin in a modest but stylish way. Melissa was in awe of its beauty, almost to the point of entrancement. She forced her eyes away but couldn't help but peer at it from the corner of her eye. It wasn't until much later that she realized it was also the only item in the booth.

"Do you like this dress, child?" Melissa nodded without raising her eyes. "It is very special and priceless with an incredible history."

"Was it yours?" Melissa asked politely, still fixated on the garment. The woman laughed.

"Heavens no. I am merely a vessel for the dress. She belongs to no one but sometimes she leads me to someone who needs her." Melissa was beginning to feel her irritability return. Great. The lady is loony.

She rose to her feet again.

"Well, it's lovely. I hope whomever she leads you to enjoys her very much." As she turned to leave, the woman began to cackle.

"The dress has chosen you, child. I thought you understood that." Melissa turned back, her brow furrowed.

"I just explained that I cannot afford this dress," she almost snapped. Crazy old bird.

"You don't need money for this but you do need to make a promise," the woman told her. Melissa paused. She was torn between wanting the intricate white creation before her and walking away from the unbalanced dame who was still speaking. Just promise her whatever she wants and run like the wind.

"Okay. I'll make a promise," Melissa finally agreed. "What is it?"

"You must promise to marry your betrothed and live out your marriage as God intended." Melissa blinked and tore her eyes away from the dress which had held her completely captive.

"Is that it?" she asked. The woman nodded.

"I promise to marry Greg and live out my marriage according to God's plan," Melissa repeated solemnly. She felt her heart skip a beat and for a split second, she was overcome by a heady, intoxicated feeling. Nodding, the older lady removed the dress from the hanger and gently wrapped it in a plastic garment bag before handing it to Melissa. Then she handed her a worn, leather-bound book.

"This comes with the dress," she told her. Then, as quickly as she had invited her into the booth, the woman was ushering her out.

"Go and live your life, child."

"Wait! What's your name?"

"You may call me Irene."

Alexandra

Melissa could not believe her good fortune. She hurried home in order to bring her precious gift to the shelter. Once inside the house, shaking off the rain, she couldn't help but wonder if she had just taken advantage of an elderly woman who had taken leave of her senses. In fact, the more Melissa thought about it, the more she realized that she had done a very foolish and possibly cruel thing. Tomorrow before work, I will go and return the dress. The old lady is probably suffering from dementia. That familiar disheartened feeling started to wash over her as she sat down on the plaid sofa and pulled off her rain boots. She shook her short blonde hair free of water droplets and stared blankly at the fireplace. I miss you, mama. I wish you were here. On impulse, Melissa threw two logs into the fireplace and lit it. Her mother used to love sitting by the fire. She would watch it for hours, lost in thought. Melissa and Michelle used to tease her about her fascination with the flames. Feeling an intense desire to be near her mom, Melissa tried to lose herself in the sparks also but she could not relax. Her head was too full to embrace a meditative state. She glanced around the room and her eyes rested on the book the old lady had bequeathed to her. Leaning forward, she picked it up. It appeared to be a journal of sorts but not written in the "Dear Diary" style. Melissa flipped to the first page. The inscription read, Alexandra, 1948.

May 4

Andrew proposed today. I suppose I should have been more excited but I was put off by his entire family being present. Where is the romance? Is our whole marriage going to be littered with his family? I don't know if I can marry a man who spends so much time with his relatives. I said "yes" but I have the sense that this engagement won't reach its fruition. He wants us to marry in the autumn.

May 9

We are barely betrothed and my future mother-in-law has already dominated the wedding plans. She insists that we have the ceremony at the Golf Club but I always wanted to marry on the beach. Andrew says I should simply let her have her way since he is her only child and she won't have an opportunity to help plan anyone else's wedding. I suppose I have no choice but to relent.

May 26

We are set to be married at the Golf Club on October 30th. Andrew's cousin Camila will be my maid of honor even though I desperately wanted my best friend Hazel to hold the title. I am quickly learning that Andrew's family always wins in these situations. I should call an end to this once and for all.

June 23

Why can't this family mind their own affairs? I feel like I can't breathe! I am constantly explaining myself to Andrew's mother on one subject or another. I don't know how much more I can take of this!

July 6

Andrew and I had a terrible argument today. He called me "cold" because I voiced my displeasure of his family's involvement in every aspect of our lives. I returned his engagement ring. I think it is best that we part ways. My heart is broken.

Unexpectedly, Melissa felt her eyes mist up. So he's close to his family. What's wrong with that? I wish that Greg were closer to his! As if on cue, there was a knock at the door. It was Greg, once again drenched from the storm. He bustled inside, shivering. He gave Melissa a peck on the cheek and smiled at her, boyishly. She was inexplicably annoyed with him.

"Why are you so late?" she demanded, glancing at the grandfather clock in the corner of the room. Greg's smile faltered and he shrugged nonchalantly.

"The job took longer than we thought. We still have more to do tomorrow." Melissa didn't reply but pursed her lips into a thin line. She suddenly understood exactly how Alexandra felt. He doesn't understand what's important to me. He's not the right man for me.

"Mel? I'm sorry about today. I know you wanted to go look at places for the wedding. But I have a feeling that this will lead to full-time employment."

"You have a feeling?" she snarled. She had no idea what had come over her. She was picking a fight but for reasons she could not comprehend. Greg looked completely perplexed by her tone.

"What's wrong?"

"Nothing. I'm just tired. It's late and I have to work tomorrow." She looked pointedly at the door. Greg turned red with humiliation.

"Are you telling me to go?" he asked incredulously. She had never thrown him out in their entire relationship. She nodded. Locking his jaw, Greg spun on his heel and headed back to the door.

"I'm doing this for us, Melissa. So you can have that all important wedding you need to have. You don't need to be so hostile." He did not wait for her reply before disappearing into the night. Sighing, she tossed another piece of firewood into the flames and plopped back down onto the sofa. She picked up the journal and continued to read.

July 30

I haven't seen or spoken to Andrew in three weeks. My heart does not want to mend. Imagine my surprise when his mother called on me this morning. I invited her in for tea. She told me that once, she had been just like me, a free spirit with an independent streak that would not be tamed. She had been shunned her own family when she had developed polio and it wasn't until Andrew's father began courting her did she understand what having people who cared about her was truly like. Soon, she had been adopted by their family and in turn, she had grown a close-knit family of her own. She told me that nothing was more important than family and sometimes, in order to keep that spirit alive, she would infringe too much in the lives of those she cared about. She apologized to me and then gave me an offering of peace; a handmade lace and satin wedding gown. She told me that it was rich in history and there was a mystery which surrounded it as it only sought out those who needed it. I couldn't stop staring at it as if I were under a spell. But she warned me that it could only be worn if I promised to live out my life with Andrew according to God's will and follow his guidance always. As I stared at that garment, all of my doubts about marrying Andrew disappeared. I agreed and embraced his mother.

Strangely, that was the final entry in the entire book, despite the fact that there were dozens more blank, browning pages within the leather binding. As Melissa flipped through the empty paper, a single business card slipped out. It read "Alexandra's Antiques" and there was a local address and phone number. Intrigued, Melissa picked up the home phone and called. The ringing was finally answered by a voice recording which stated the store's hours. Melissa slowly replaced the receiver. I'll have to go there one day and meet Alexandra.

Melissa woke at dawn the following morning and carefully wrapped the wedding dress into another plastic bag and then placed it in a brown paper bag along with the diary. She got dressed for work and headed out to the market. The cursed rain had yet to cease. It had been three days of gray, depressing weather. Regardless, she vowed to return the dress to Irene. She didn't feel right having taken it from such an obviously feeble-minded woman. Yet on the bus ride, she re-read the passage where Alexandra's mother-in-law to be explains the importance of the ceremonial attire. She had verbatim said what Irene had said. Oh pshaw. Irene probably wrote the journal herself.

As Melissa disembarked the bus, she looked around, attempting to recall where Irene's booth had been. She remembered it was in an obscure spot she had never seen before but after an hour of wandering the marketplace, she was unable to locate the old woman and her stand. In fact, she couldn't even find the area she had stumbled upon the previous day. Feeling guilty, Melissa returned to the bus stop. As she waited for the line which would take her to work, she suddenly realized that she was mere blocks from the spot where Alexandra's Antique's was located. On a whim, she decided to visit the store.

It took her less than ten minutes to get there and when she arrived, she was pleasantly surprised by a small, old brick structure displaying antique toys and relics from all walks of life. She opened the door, a chime announcing her arrival and hurried inside. As her eyes adjusted to the dimness of the store, she eagerly looked at the counter, completely expecting Irene to be there. To her disappointment, a young man, just barely out of his teens was leaning over the counter, playing on his laptop. He completely ruined the old fashioned energy which had embraced her. Sullenly, Melissa turned to leave but the man-boy called out.

"May I help you, miss?" His polite demeanor surprised her. She paused and turned back to him.

"No...I...well maybe. Is this Alexandra's Antiques?" she asked, feeling witless as the words left her lips. The young man smiled welcomingly.

"Yes. Can I help you find something?"

"No...I...well...I'm looking for Alexandra." The boy's smile faltered.

"I'm sorry, miss. My mom is quite ill and in the hospital. Are you a friend?" Melissa was aghast at her own stupidity. Of course, the Alexandra from the book could not have been his mother. The boy was much too young. It was merely a coincidence that the store was named the same name. Melissa shook her head and began to back out of the store. As she did, she backed into a small decorative table by the cash counter and a frame fell over. Thankfully it did not break.

"Oh! I'm sorry!" She picked up the photo hastily and then froze. "Who is this?"

The boy gave the picture a quick glance.

"Oh, that's my mom's mom. Actually, her name was Alexandra too." He smiled a faraway smile. "Before she died, she used to have all of us over for supper every single Sunday, even when it got to be over twenty-five cousins jand grandkids. She would make quilts for all the kids. She taught everyone how to bake. And she was always in everyone's business. Nothing happened in our family without Grandma Alex knowing about it. She really was the glue who kept us all together." His eyes clouded over for a moment and he cleared his throat. Melissa nodded slowly and carefully put the frame back onto the small podium but not before she took one last glance at Alexandra and Andrew's wedding photo. Alexandra was instantly recognizable, wearing an ecstatic smile and the mystical dress that Melissa was carrying in a paper bag.

Elyse

Melissa did something she never did; she called in sick to work as soon as she walked out of the store. She was awash with a sea of emotions she could not comprehend and she felt like she needed to go home and be alone with her thoughts. Once she slipped over the threshold into the house, she carefully removed the dress from its packaging and stared at it. Again, it seemed to have a hypnotic affect on her. She placed it over the couch and sat down, idly stroking the cover of the book. She wondered how Alexandra had adopted such a different outlook after feeling so strongly about Andrew's family. She opened the diary to read the words she had already almost completely committed to memory. To her complete shock, the writing was no longer Alexandra's. In its place was an even, feminine scrawl which read Elyse, 1962. Confused, Melissa thumbed through the pages, individually, but Alexandra's words were gone as if they had never been there in the first place. She rubbed her eyes in disbelief and began to read.

April 14

Sam and I are getting hitched! Hee haw! It's about time! He proposed at the protest and everyone cheered. It was the most romantic thing in the world. I can't wait to spend the rest of my life with him! We have decided to elope. We're too broke to have a big wedding. His mom hates me anyway so I can't wait to see the look on her face when we tell her we got married behind her back. His brother is going to be a witness and my sister. We're doing it next month. Going upstate and finding a little church in the country. It is going to be the most beautiful ceremony. I can hardly wait!

April 20

We are looking at houses for sale. Sam said that we need at least four bedrooms for the children. He's such a joker. We aren't having kids. We don't need anyone else but us.

May 1

I think Sam genuinely wants to start a family. He keeps making little jokes about it but I sense a truth behind his words. I wonder if we're doing the right thing. I don't want to disappoint him but I don't want children. I thought he understood that.

May 10

We are leaving on Friday for upstate. Sam's brother took him out for his bachelor party and Sam's sister-in-law Mary came to stay with me and my sister. She brought her daughter and son along. They were such good, well-behaved children for ones so young. They were nothing like how my sister and I were at that age. Mary also brought me a gorgeous gift. It was the most spectacular wedding gown I have ever seen. It looks so expensive and Mary told me that there is a colorful history surrounding it. She warned me that it can only be worn if I promise to live my life with Sam according to God's plan and after I set eyes on it, I would have agreed to anything she made me promise. I can't think of a better way to become Mrs. Samuel Boswell.

Once again, the book came to an abrupt end. No further entries. Nothing to hint at what may have happened to Elyse. Well, I guess I'm going to have to find out for myself. Melissa pulled out the phone book and began looking for Boswell. To her surprise, there were a mere four listings but only one of them was S. Boswell. Before she could stop herself, Melissa was dialing the number at her fingers. Hang up! What are you doing? But before her hands could obey her brain, someone breathlessly answered the phone.

"Hello!"

"Uh...hi...is Elyse Boswell home?"

"Yep! Mom! Mom? It's for you!"

There was a click as someone picked up the extension.

"Hello?"

"Not you, idiot! It's for mom. MOM!" There was a click as the second person replaced the receiver. A moment later there was another click.

"Hello?" a young girl this time.

"Are you people deaf? IT'S FOR MOM! Are you mom? Hang up the phone, stupid face!" And then there was silence as both parties hung up in Melissa's ear. So she married him and had three children...at least? Melissa looked back at the dress. Was the garment God's way of ensuring the women who wore it lived happy, fulfilled lives? She turned back to the book. She hadn't even closed it yet like before with Alexandra, the careful script that Elyse had written was gone. And Melissa was staring at someone else's words.

Amber

This one was harder to read as the writing was nearly illegible. But Melissa pulled her lids into slits and surged through, anxious to read the next story.

Amber, 1997

March 11

The day is getting closer! I have no idea what I'm going to do for a dress! We went way over budget with the dj and bar. My mom says I can wear her dress but it is ugly! I didn't tell her that though. She's still mad I refuse to get married in a church. She doesn't understand that Eddy and I are atheists. I only have three weeks left to find something!

March 19th

Wow! I found the most amazing dress in a trunk in grandma's attic. She says she has no idea how it got there but she told me she doesn't like it for me. She begged me not to wear it for some reason. Old people are weird. I don't care. I need a dress and it's a perfect fit. A little old fashioned maybe but still beautiful. I'm getting married! Yay!

That was it. Two chicken scratched scribbles and absolutely nothing else…except…as Melissa sifted through the book, a small square of paper slipped out and onto her lap. All of the blood rushed out of her face when she realized what she was holding. It was Amber's obituary. Dead at thirty-two. She shouldn't have worn the dress, Melissa thought mournfully, taking in the woman's dark eyes and shiny hair. She had no intention of following God's plan and look what happened. Shaken to her core, Melissa stood up, trembling, trying to gather her thoughts. Dear Lord, what does this mean? Am I to marry Greg regardless of how many doubts I have? She suddenly was desperate to see Greg. She flung open the door and a clap of thunder made her jump. Steadying her nerves, she ran down the street to his house and pounded on the door. His mother answered and told her that he was still at the construction site. Running now, Melissa caught the bus as it turned the corner and headed toward downtown. Shivering, she huddled in the back of the near empty vessel. When the droplets on her face dried, she looked up and was staring into the gray eyes of the woman she had encountered earlier in the week. The woman opened her mouth to say something but was interrupted as someone shouted,

"Elyse? Elyse Boswell? Is that you? How the heck is Sam? How are the kids?" The woman looked at the man calling for attention and Melissa suddenly felt everything in her world connect.

She scurried the ten blocks from the bus stop to the job site where Greg was just packing up with the crew. He looked concerned as he saw her approaching.

"Melissa, are you – ?"

She flung herself into his arms and kissed him warmly.

"I'm fine. I just wanted to be near you." Greg looked touched by her words. He stared at her hopefully.

"Hey, guess what? They hired me on full time starting Monday!"

"That's amazing, sweetheart. I love you, Gregory Bond. I don't care where we get married or how we get married, as long as we are together.

There is nothing we can't overcome together." His face broke into a huge grin and he returned her embrace.

"I love you too, Melissa Bond."

For the first time in three days, the rain abruptly came to a complete stop and the sun parted the dismal clouds as if God himself was pre-blessing their nuptials.

Melissa

How strange to have found such a lovely gown in a dumpster and yet that is exactly where the homeless lady claimed she had discovered the satin and lace attire. The timing could not have been better. Lisette was running out of time to find a dress and the pressure of the wedding was affecting both she and Daniel. They were bickering constantly, often over the pettiest subjects and while they were both aware of this, they seemed unable to stop. Things were getting worse and Lisette found herself questioning their relationship more and more. The bag lady had made a prophetic statement before handing her the dress outside the 7-11.

"You can wear have this dress but you must always follow God's will in your marriage. Do you promise?" Lisette had nodded vehemently and promised. With the dress had come a beat up leather bound book as well. When she arrived home, Lisette quickly tried on the dress for size and was thrilled to find it fit perfectly as if it were made for her. Then she turned to the book and opened it up. It read Melissa, 2016.

HER HUSBAND, THE SOLDIER

MARNIE PAUL

Chapter 1

Jessie Wilcox looked around the fancy new restaurant in town. Arthur Orlando, her longtime boyfriend and assumed fiancé, had wanted to bring her to this new place. He said that he wanted to show her off and give her a nice evening at the same time. Jessie was used to nice restaurants, but there was always something about them that made her feel uncomfortable. Her parents had brought her up to use the right forks and glasses, so it wasn't that. "We will have no Wilcox making a fool of herself in public!" They had said.

As Jessie picked at her second course, she kept thinking about how she should be back at her dorm studying for the mid-terms coming up. This was her last semester, and she couldn't believe she would be graduating in nine weeks.

"Jessica," Arthur said, taking her hand from across the table. "You seem a bit distracted. Could it be that something is bothering you?"

Jessie shrugged. "I know I should be studying. I know the material, but I can't help thinking that going over it one more time will help seal it in."

Arthur shook his head. "Why do you worry about such things? I never understood your reason for wanting to attend college anyway. You know that I have more than enough money for us to use however we want. I certainly hope you are not thinking of becoming employed after you finish."

They had had similar conversations before, and Jessie knew that Arthur frowned upon her idea of making her own living. She wanted some sort of purpose, not to just be living off the money her parents had or her boyfriend had. She wasn't even sure what she felt for Arthur or if she wanted to be with him. But because both sets of their parents expected it, Jessie went along with him as it was easier than making a big scene.

Jessie declined to answer and instead, shoveled food into her mouth as a cover-up. "I think this new restaurant must have an excellent cook," Jessie said when she had finished chewing.

Arthur nodded, distracted from the subject of her wanting to get a job. "His name is Antwan, and he has had training at the Institute of Culinary Education in New York. That is one of the best schools in this country, and I can always catch that unique taste their top cooks have."

Jessie was not surprised by Arthur's knowledge on the cook's background. That was typical for him. He frowned upon her knowledge of the country's history or periodic table, but he could know everything about everyone, and it was perfectly fine. Jessie simply nodded and appeared properly impressed.

"For someone who must earn a living, a profession such as being a cook is an excellent choice. It provides opportunity to rise. Perhaps, if this cook has enough practice, he could become the personal cook for someone like you or me."

Jessie hated the insinuation that someone like herself or Arthur were better than the average person, but she knew there was no use trying to change him.

"Now," Arthur said, "I was thinking that after we finish dinner, we could go to the country club for an evening of drinks."

"Arthur," Jessie protested as all possibility of her studying seemed to be vanishing. "I really should get back after we finish dinner."

He shook his head and forced his will on her. "You don't even need a college education. I don't know why you push yourself so hard when there are many other ways of entertainment. You should really relax a bit more."

Jessie remained quiet rather than making a scene. After they finished dinner, Arthur drove them over to the country club. He made the rounds, greeting their acquaintances with her on his arm, but she didn't say much. She really wanted to get back to her studying, but she didn't know how else to say it.

"I'm going to get myself something to drink," Jessie said. "Would you like anything?"

"I'm fine at the moment," Arthur said, indicating the drink in he already had in his hand. Jessie went over to the bar to escape Arthur's scrutiny. While she knew a majority of the people in the bar, she couldn't say she was really friends with all of them or even any of them. As Jessie imagined herself married to Arthur and doing this for the rest of her life, she began to feel sick. No way could she be happy!

When it was getting late, Jessie was finally able to pull Arthur away from his friends and convince him to drive her back to college. He was pretty tipsy, and Jessie ended up driving for fear that they would have an accident.

"Do you want some water or something?" Jessie asked before she got out of the driver's seat. "Or perhaps you'd like to just rest for a little while."

"No, I'm fine," Arthur insisted. "I don't know why you thought you needed to drive. I'm not drunk; I've just had a bit of wine."

Jessie shrugged and handed him the keys. "It's all yours," she said, glad that she had gotten to her dorm safely.

"I'll call you later," Arthur said. "We can- go out again," he seemed to forget what he was saying as he was saying it. He repeated it again to make sure she had heard. "We can go out again."

Jessie nodded, and Arthur tried to kiss her. Jessie endured the kiss then went into the safety of her dorm. She was past exhausted and knew there was no way she would be able to study. Jessie hoped she had enough knowledge to pass the mid-term on her own.

Chapter 2

After Jessie had finished all of her mid-terms that week, she felt as though she deserved some relaxing. In Jessie's mind, a carton of ice cream was what she needed. She also wanted to pick up some snacks for her dorm room.

She started moseying down the frozen food aisle, peering into the freezers and seeing what kinds were available. She paused in front of one. She was just bending forward to pull the door open when the door of the freezer next to her came flying out and smacked her in the head. Jessie stumbled back, slipped, and fell on her bottom. She would have been embarrassed, but her head hurt so badly that Jessie couldn't think about anything else.

"Oh my god, are you okay?" a voice asked. Jessie shook her head as the pain pounded through it. Her eyes were squeezed shut as she tried to stop the stars she was seeing.

"Okay, just lay down," the voice commanded. "I'll grab one of these frozen things for an ice pack. Keep your eyes closed." It felt strange to Jessie as she automatically obeyed each of the male stranger's commands.

She felt a rough hand slowly moving her hand from her forehead and placing something frozen there instead. Jessie's hand automatically went up to sustain the frozen package, and it landed on the rough hand. She started to move her own, but the voice stopped her. "No, you'd better hold that on there. I'm going to get the manager and see if we need to call an ambulance. Stay right here."

It had just been a knock to the head, but waves of pain were pounding through Jessie's temple. She felt like a little girl at that moment. She wanted to cry out and stop the voice from leaving, but she knew she couldn't. She heard more voices bending over her, making comments or asking questions. Jessie ignored them all until she heard the first voice coming back.

"It seems that I hit her pretty hard on the head with the door. I wasn't looking," he said. "But I don't know if it's serious. She could have a concussion. It might not be that serious."

"How do you feel?" a female voice asked Jessie.

She spoke for the first time since the accident. "My head really hurts."

"What's your name?"

"Jessica."

"What day is it?"

"March 24th," Jessie answered.

Jessie tried to crack her eyes open, and she got a shattered view of everything around her. She saw the manager bending over her. "I'm going to touch your head and tell me if it hurts," she said. She gently probed around Jessie's forehead, and only one spot was sore.

"Do you have someone who can take you home?" the manager asked. "I know you are not safe to drive, but I believe if you can lay down and rest, you will feel a bit better. You might have a bit of a bump for a while, but you definitely don't have a concussion."

"Um," Jessie's mind fumbled for someone who could drive her home. She didn't dare call Arthur or she would hear about this accident for the rest of her life. Her mind scrambled. "I do have one friend I can call." Jessie called her roommate, but the phone just rang and rang. "I don't think she's there," Jessie said, cracking her eyes open again to get a glimpse of the scene.

"That's alright," the first voice jumped back in. Jessie thought that voice had left and gone about his business. "I can drive her home."

Jessie felt a little nervous about riding back to her dorm with a stranger, but she didn't know what other choice she had. The voice finally came into her view, and she saw that it was attached to a man in a Marine uniform. For some reason, upon seeing that, Jessie felt a little more soothed. He was a Marine. He worked to protect the country. He must not have any qualms about protecting individual citizens either.

"Thank you," she said. "I don't even know if I can walk."

"Let's try it," the Marine said. "By the way, I'm Thomas. Brenda, can you get on her other side? Actually, let me pull my car around first, then we can get her to the front door. It won't be as far."

"Alright," Brenda, the manager, said. "I'll wait right here with her." Jessie waited anxiously with the package of frozen food still plastered to her forehead. While Thomas was gone, Brenda wrapped the frozen food in a small washcloth and gave it back to her. "That won't be so cold now, especially on your hands."

"Alright," Jessie heard Thomas's voice. "Let's go."

Jessie stumbled to her feet, with one of the on either side of her. She knew she probably looked foolish, like a drunk person about to be thrown out of the frat party. She opened her eyes a slit so that she could help a little bit with the walking part.

Finally, they were going out the sliding glass doors into the frosty air. She saw a car sitting right on the curb. Thomas opened the back door, and Jessie briefly wondered if he was going to kidnap her. She realized that she had no reason to doubt him and laid down on the backseat with Brenda's help.

"Thank you, sir," Brenda said, nodding at Thomas. "You have done more than required to in the situation, and you are welcome back here anytime." Brenda also said something to Jessie about hoping she recovered quickly.

"Where do you live?" Thomas asked, sliding into the driver's seat. Jessie was so pleased with the darkness of the backseat that she was able to open her eyes almost all the way.

"I live on North Campus of Harvard."

"You're a student at Harvard?" Thomas asked, starting the car.

"Yes, I'm almost done. I only have a few more weeks."

"Well, congratulations," Thomas said.

Jessie cleared her throat and found herself wanting to converse further with this gentleman. "Why did you become a Marine?"

"Truthfully, it was my only option after high school. I knew I could either keep working a minimum wage job at McDonald's or go into the Marines. I didn't have enough money or a way to get financing to go to college, so that was out."

"How long have you been in the Marines?" Jessie asked.

"This is my sixth year," Thomas answered.

"Do you get stationed out of the country a lot?"

"I've been out two different times, each for about fifteen to eighteen months. Right now, I'm stationed on base here."

"What's it like. . .over there, if I can ask?"

"Of course," Thomas answered gently. "And I'll be honest. It's difficult. We see families, especially children with so much need. Our job is to protect the country, but we can't help but become emotionally involved with the natives around us. Most of the time, no one in our division knows the language, but we get by somehow. I feel really sorry for them, and I like that I get to protect them. I feel like protecting them gives me a purpose, you know? I'm not just living for the next fun thing; I'm actually doing something worth doing."

Jessie was quiet as she heard Thomas's answer. She wished she could hear something like that from Arthur.

"Do you plan on always being in the Marines?"

"I didn't," Thomas said. "I signed on originally for three years. But when that time came up, I had just finished my first time serving in Vietnam. I wanted to do something else. I signed on for another four years. I don't know what I'll do after that."

"Do you *want* to continue?"

"Yeah," Thomas said. "I really do, but I don't know." Thomas laughed suddenly. "Here I am, working through my future life options with you, a stranger, who I am taking to her home. Life always has a curveball to throw, doesn't it?"

Jessie nodded then realized he couldn't see her nod. "Yes, I certainly didn't expect a quick stop at the grocery store to turn out like this."

"I didn't either," Thomas said. "I'm really sorry, by the way. I really did not look where I was flinging the door."

Jessie laughed, and the noise hurt her head. "That's okay. I usually don't look either. This is just payback for the time I accidentally hit a toddler with a door."

"Lousy payback," Thomas said. "I should turn in here, right?"

"Oh, ah," Jessie tried to sit up and glare through the blaring lights of the night, but she couldn't see anything clearly. "I'm sorry. I really can't see. It hurts my head too much."

"Right, yeah. The sign I just passed said North Campus, but I don't know if it meant the turn right after it or this one coming up."

"Either one," Jessie said. "My building should have the number 120 on it. Sorry I can't be more help, but the lights are really hurting my head."

"No, no, it's fine," Thomas assured her. "It may take me a bit longer, but I'll find it."

"You don't have anywhere you have to be?" Jessie asked.

"No, I'm off duty tonight. Don't worry."

The car was silent as Thomas drove, trying to locate the right building. "I think I found it. 120 you said?"

"Yeah, that's it," Jessie said, wondering how she was going to walk inside.

"Don't get out by yourself," Thomas said. "Give me just a minute, and I'll get you." Jessie lay patiently, feeling as though she could lay in the same place for an eternity. It felt so comfortable. She felt the door by her feet open. "Okay, try to get down if you can, and I'll be here to catch you."

Jessie was thankful that she was not wearing a dress as she slithered toward the open door, her eyes still half shut. As her bottom reached the seat edge, she gave a wiggle, and her feet descended until they hit the pavement. She squeezed her eyes shut as a jolt of pain passed through. She felt Thomas's hands on her hips as she stumbled forward and pressed against him.

She straightened up and opened her eyes most of the way. As soon as she did, she looked right into Thomas's grey eyes for the first time. They sent a shockwave through her just as powerful as any of the pain she had felt due to her head injury. She felt as though she could not breath, and she took a step backward.

"Are you alright? I didn't mean for you to come down quite that hard," Thomas said, his hands still firmly on her.

"Yeah, yeah, I'm fine," Jessie assured, making a grab for her purse. Thomas grabbed it first, and Jessie had a brief moment of wondering if he was going to steal it from her, then she shook that from her mind. Of course not!

"I'll just walk you in," Thomas said.

Chapter 3

"How did you find yourself a soldier?" Hallie asked.

Jessie shook her head. "He's a Marine," she said, eyes closed as she lay on her bed, listening to her roommate's questions. "And if you had answered when I called, he wouldn't have needed to bring me all the way here."

"Who would have wanted to miss that?" Hallie asked. "I get that you're in a lot of pain, but he's pretty cute in case you didn't notice."

Jessie shrugged. "I have Arthur, remember?" she really did not want to get into this conversation, but Hallie was clearly interested.

"Arthur is a prig. I don't know why you're still with him. I mean, sure, you can get into some fancy places with him, but I don't think that's worth sacrificing your love life."

Jessie didn't feel like explaining that with her family's name and money, she could get into those places anyway. She just never went without Arthur, because she didn't find them entertaining.

"I'll do my life, and you do yours. I think that's a good plan," Jessie said.

"Whatever, I'm just saying. I may use that phone number he gave you if you're not going to."

"It's not for calling him up to date," Jessie smiled despite herself. "He gave it to me in case I need to be checked out by a doctor. He said he would pay for it."

"Still, I think that's pretty sweet of him," Hallie said. "But, suit yourself. Pass up on such a wonderful opportunity and spend the rest of your life going to awesome places with terrible company."

Hallie turned back to her homework, but Jessie couldn't stop thinking about her words. She knew she didn't love Arthur, but it was easier for everyone if she just went along with it. But could she go along with it forever? Even if she did decide she didn't want to spend the rest of her life with Arthur, that didn't give her license to chase down the kindly gentleman in the grocery store. He was simply being nice, and he hadn't meant anything else.

But even as she tried, Jessie couldn't forget about this Thomas. About a week later, she got a phone call from the very Thomas.

"I just wanted to call and make sure you were okay," Thomas said.

By now, Jessie had no pain, and she wondered if that night hadn't been a bit exaggerated or if she had really felt that much pain at the time. "I'm fine. Really. It was just a knock to the head, and I barely even remember it now."

"Oh no, are you losing your memory because of it?"

Jessie laughed. "No, I mean, it was no big deal." She took a deep breath, going out on a limb. "I want to. . .thank you for your kindness. Perhaps I could take you out for ice cream. That's what I was going to the store to buy anyway."

Thomas was silent, and Jessie wondered if he was going to turn her down with a flat no. "Sure, but I'm on duty the next two nights. What about Friday?"

"That sounds great. I'll see you at Sunni Skies on Friday then."

Jessie hung up the phone, and she couldn't help but feel excited. This did not count as cheating on Arthur. She was merely saying thank you for a stranger's unexpected kindness. Arthur would do the same if he had known about the incident. Fortunately, Jessie had convinced Hallie not to say a word about any of it. Jessie thought Arthur might be angry that she hadn't called him.

When Friday night came, Jessie dressed casually, as she had been when she went grocery shopping. This wasn't even a date. They were just getting ice cream. Thomas confirmed the time with her, and Jessie arrived early. She got out of her car and waited by the front door. The porch on the family-run business was packed with customers. Maye Friday night had not been the most discrete night to get ice cream.

"Hey," Thomas said, tapping her on the shoulder.

Jessie turned around and felt that same spark in her stomach that she had when they met. "Hey. Do you want to go inside?"

After spending so much time imagining what they would talk about or if they would even have anything to say, Jessie was finding her words awkward and stilted.

"I'm always surprised by all the flavors here," Thomas said as he studied the menu.

Jessie looked through the glass as the featured flavors up front. "Do you come here often?"

"Not too much," Thomas shrugged. "We're encouraged to stay in shape, but I'm not in basic anymore, so they're not as dictatorial."

"Good, cause as a college student, I like to treat myself as often as possible. I don't come here as much as I should, though."

They both ordered and received their cones. "Let's sit outside," Thomas suggested. "There are too many people inside."

Jessie agreed, and the two found one of the many bench swings available. They sat down, and Jessie began swaying the swing absentmindedly with her foot as they licked away. "I must say, this is one of the most delicious thank yous I may have ever received," Thomas teased.

"Well," Jessie said. "Some people may have walked away if they had done what you did. I mean, not that you did anything really bad. I know it was an accident, but. . ."

Thomas stopped her. "Hey, no big deal. It's in the past. It doesn't matter." Thomas took a few licks from his cone before he re-started the conversation. "What are you getting your degree in?"

"I'm getting my degree in human services. I've interned with a foster care center, and I think I might work with that same center once I have my actual degree."

"What kind of work do they do?"

"They work with helping make sure that the kids who have been given foster families are being properly cared for. That mostly means that I would be checking up on families, interviewing kids, making sure that everything is as it should be. If any families are interested in beginning foster care, I would be responsible for training them. That sort of thing."

"Are you into adoption and fostering? I mean, would you consider doing it?"

Jessie shrugged. "I don't think so." She tried to think of Arthur adopting a child, and she couldn't even begin to make the picture. "I mean, I think it's a great idea, but I don't know that I'll do it myself. I prefer to help others who can better provide for them."

Thomas nodded. "That's great. You know, I'm a Christian. I don't know how you feel about God and faith in him, but I know that it has changed me. I was adopted when I was six years old. My family didn't have a lot of money, but they taught me how to love God. That was a much better gift than anything they could have given me monetarily."

Jessie studied him as she momentarily forgot about her ice cream. Here, sitting beside her, was the very product of the work she was doing with foster children. The children she saw into foster homes, who were sometimes adopted into those homes, could turn into young Marines who helped hurt strangers in the grocery store.

"It's good to know my work may help some kids, you know?" Jessie said, her eyes still fixed on Thomas's.

Thomas nodded slowly, and before Jessie even knew what she was doing, her lips were on Thomas's. They were kissing, and Jessie did not wake from her dream until she felt the cold drips of the ice cream on her hand. She wiped them away with a napkin then dared to look at Thomas again. He was smiling.

Then, he bit his lip and nodded. "I kind of like you, Jessie," he said.

Jessie smiled widely. When Thomas came in for another kiss, she turned her mouth up toward his.

Chapter 4

"I have to break up with Arthur," Jessie told her roommate. "It's not fair. I definitely feel something for Thomas. I feel like I'm cheating, but then, I feel like I was never emotionally involved with Arthur anyway, so it doesn't feel like real cheating."

"I'm pretty sure there is not a category of fake cheating," Hallie cut in. "So, any kind of cheating would be real. But seriously, break up with Arthur. He is a jerk, and Thomas seems to be a real gentleman. I don't get why you even have any qualms about it. I would have already broken up with Arthur if it was me."

Jessie nodded. "I know. That's what my head is telling me."

"But. . .?"

"But, I barely know Thomas. I think I like him, but that doesn't mean anything will come of it. Besides, if I break up with Arthur, I'm pretty sure my parents will kill me."

"Now, I get why you are with him," Hallie nodded. "Your parents see something in him. Look, do what you want. You'll be marrying whoever you choose, not your parents, so you better like him."

Jessie nodded. "Yeah, I'm going to do it. Just not today."

Hallie shook her head. "Thomas will be really annoyed at you if he finds out you have a boyfriend, so you better do it soon or you could lose Thomas."

Jessie backed away from the window. "I'll do something before the weekend." The weekend was still three days away, and Jessie was so wrapped up in her last semester of school, that she knew making a decision before then would be too rushed. "I'm going to see Thomas again."

"When?"

"Tomorrow. Maybe, that can help me make a decision."

"I think you already know what you're going to do," Hallie advised. "Doing it sooner than later can save you from any extra problems."

"Thanks, Missie. Someday, I'll try to be as rational as you." Jessie shook her head, but she didn't tell Hallie that she had been texting Thomas as often as he could. They'd even talked on the phone a few times. She was surprised that he wanted to take her out tonight. He said his buddies were going to the bar, and he didn't want to get drunk. He preferred to do something else. Jessie's admiration for him was growing by the day, no, by the hour.

This time, Jessie dressed up a little more nicely. She might as well dress to impress. She was pretty sure Thomas was interested in her if his kisses meant anything. She didn't dare go on the Marine base to see him, but she waited until he had enough time off that he could set up a time for them to go out.

"Wow," Thomas said when he saw her. "You look. . .amazing."

"Thanks," Jessie said, his words making her glow. Jessie somehow felt as though his words were not calculated to get her into bed later but because he genuinely thought them. "You look pretty good yourself."

"Shall we go in?" Thomas had chosen a nice restaurant, but nothing like the kind of place Jessie went with Arthur. It was nice to look at the menu and order something greasy for once instead of some dainty dish she couldn't pronounce.

They ordered their food, and as they were waiting for it, Thomas decided they would play a little game. "I'm sure you've played it before, but it'll tell me two things. First, I'll learn more about you. Secondly, I'll learn if you're a good liar or not."

"If I'm a good liar, is that a bad thing?" Jessie teased. "I either lose the game or risk you thinking me a good liar. That's not much of a choice."

Thomas shrugged. "Go ahead." The couple played two truths and a lie, and Jessie was able to trick Thomas a fair amount of the time.

"You're not related to the Wilcox family that's big in this town are you?" Thomas asked.

Jessie bit her lip. She didn't want him to see her as a bank. Her parents had warned her against guys like that, but there was something about Thomas that made Jessie doubt he would be like that. "Yes," she nodded slowly. "I am."

Thomas shrugged. "Yeah, I kept hearing the name around town. And the guys would talk about it. I just wondered. So, I guess you're from here, then."

"Yes," Jessie nodded. "I've grown up here."

The two ate their meal, and Jessie couldn't help thinking about when they would share their next kiss. Their first had been so special that she just wanted another. Jessie was becoming distracted during the meal, and Thomas seemed to sense it.

"Are you okay? There's no delayed concussion is there?"

Jessie smiled and shook her head. "No. I've just got a lot on my mind."

"What is it?" Thomas asked. Jessie wanted to tell him everything, but she was afraid that he would judge her for not breaking up with Arthur or being straight with him before. Jessie shook her head and focused on the food instead. When they finished, they found a bench outside the restaurant and sat down. Jessie wasn't quite ready to end the night, and Thomas seemed to feel the same.

When they sat down, Jessie kept looking at Thomas's lips. He seemed to get her hint and leaned in to kiss her gently. He slid his hand to the nape of her neck and kissed her ever so gently. When he pulled back, Jessie laid her head on his shoulder. Being with Thomas definitely felt right.

"I wanted to talk to you about something," Thomas said after they had been silent for several moments. Thomas intertwined his fingers with Jessie's, and she sat up so that she could see his face. "I've just gotten notice that I'm going to be shipped back to Vietnam in three weeks."

His words hit Jessie hard. "You- you're going away. How long?"

"Twelve months," Thomas said. Suddenly, the reality of being with someone in the Marines hit Jessie hard. She nodded, stood, and fled to her car.

Chapter 5

Safely in her car, Jessie began to cry. Her relationship with Thomas had been too perfect. He was too perfect. Of course, fate wouldn't allow her to be happy. She would be stuck with Arthur for her whole life, going to all these social functions that she never wanted to attend. A sudden relief hit Jessie that she hadn't broken up with Arthur and caused a scene. She had been right to do what she did.

An hour later, when Jessie saw that she was getting a call from Thomas, she went outside to answer it in privacy.

"I'm sorry," Thomas said, as soon as she answered. "I shouldn't have told you like that. I shouldn't have kissed you. That only made it worse. I honestly didn't know before today, or I would have told you before. I never expected to feel so strongly about you."

His words did nothing to make Jessie feel better, and she only cried harder. Then, she heard something she hadn't expected to hear. It sounded like Thomas was crying! Jessie tried to stem her tears to hear for sure, but she couldn't be certain. "I didn't mean to walk away from you," Jessie tried to apologize. "I mean, I did, but I don't know why I did. I just felt like you tricked me."

"I didn't trick you, and I never misled you," Thomas said, his voice definitely thick with emotion. "I didn't mean to start anything with you, but then, I don't know. Maybe you don't even feel anything for me, but I know that I. . . feel something for you. I don't really know what."

"Why don't you come over here, and we can talk," Jessie said, wanting to feel his arms around her.

"I don't think that's a good idea," Thomas said. "I think, it'll only make us both more emotional, and people don't really make wise decisions when they are emotional." Did he think that she was. . .? Jessie didn't know what she was trying to do, but his words just felt like another rejection.

"I'm sorry," Thomas said. "I can talk tomorrow night if you want. We can go to Sunni Skies again." The idea of pretending that nothing had happened and going to get ice cream as they had before seemed appealing, and Jessie agreed.

That night she could think of nothing other than Thomas. What were her options? Love him and be away from him for a year? Or be with Arthur in a miserable relationship where he would be there for her as much as she wanted?

When Jessie arrived at Sunni Skies, she was following all the tricks she knew not to cry upon seeing Thomas. She hurried into his arms and hugged him tightly. "I missed you," she said, the words slipping out of her mouth. They didn't make sense. She had seen him only the night before. Maybe she meant she would miss him.

"Let's get some ice cream," Thomas said. "It's on me."

After getting their cones, Jessie snuggled up to Thomas and licked her ice cream without speaking. "I know it would be hard," Thomas said, "And I don't want to make you do anything you don't want to, but I'd love to stay in contact with you while I am there. We can email as much as we want, and I would even be able to Skype sometimes. I don't want to lose you though."

Jessie took a shuddering sigh. "But, it would be a whole year. I've only known you a month," Jessie said. Their foundation for a long distance relationship was shaky. She didn't know him well enough to know if she wanted to commit to that.

"It doesn't have to be a titled relationship," Thomas said, "I get it. It's a long time. You barely know me, but I am confident in how I feel for you."

Jessie sat up and turned around to look into his eyes. "How- how do you feel about me?"

Thomas smiled. "Like God had a hand in my hitting you in the grocery store."

"So God made you open the door so forcefully that it hit an innocent bystander on the head?"

Thomas nodded. "Yes, so that our lives would be forever changed." He glanced at her lips, and Jessie knew he wanted to kiss her. But, she really didn't need anything else confusing her at the moment.

"Where would we be if I had decided not to go to the grocery store that day?" Jessie asked aloud.

"We probably wouldn't be eating ice cream together. We wouldn't have met," Thomas answered, though the same answers were already running through Jessie's mind.

Jessie knew that Thomas would fil her life with love even if he wouldn't be at her side the whole time. Eventually, he would be. "What happens when you come back?" Jessie asked.

"We pick up where we left off," Thomas said. "And this assignment would be my last. When my next contract is over, I can get a job here. We could be together."

The thought filled Jessie with so much joy that she couldn't think of anything else. "Okay," she said, nodding.

"Okay to what?" Thomas asked.

"Okay, I want to talk to you while you're gone. I want to know everything about your life there, and I want to learn more about you."

Thomas leaned down and kissed Jessie with his caramel flavored lips. "Okay, then. Let's do it."

* 9 7 9 8 2 2 4 3 5 0 4 0 7 *